AMISH BACHELOR'S CHRISTMAS

BOOK 3 AMISH CHRISTMAS BOOKS

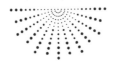

SAMANTHA PRICE

CHAPTER ONE

Joe sat alone, isolated in his uncle's cottage not sure he'd made the right move. He'd put himself into this situation when his parents nearly begged him to be the stand-in bishop at Stinterton, a town in the middle of nowhere. Granted, it had been his decision in the end, but what could he say when they told him his uncle said he was the only man who could do it? Just before he said yes, he spoke to Uncle Luke, who mentioned he could always ask Samson. Joe told him there was no need to do that, he'd go.

There had always been some kind of unhealthy competitiveness between him and Samson, his cousin on his father's side. He was the only one in the family who could see through Samson—knew his true nature. Whenever Samson had visited his community when they were young, Samson had tried his best to put Joe in a bad light and it had worked to a certain degree. Back then Samson was seen as bright and clever, whereas Joe was known as a troublemaker, a borderline delinquent, and someone who didn't quite follow the rules. He couldn't help feeling that as adults nothing had changed.

Joe shrugged the images of Samson from his mind. It was bad enough he was in this tiny isolated town with nothing to do and nowhere to go, he didn't want to make it worse by thinking about his cousin. If all went to plan, he'd never have to lay eyes on Samson again.

The thought of the small town was far better than the reality. The town, if you could call it that, wasn't much. Just one general store that doubled as the post office and town business administration center, that sold everything from food and household supplies to generators and hardware. The one other business was next door to the store, a house that had been converted into a café and takeout food outlet.

When Joe arrived yesterday, he'd wanted to turn around and leave, but he couldn't because that would reinforce everyone's perception of him as unreliable. He wasn't. He needed to change their perception so he had to stay put.

He was here until his uncle recovered in an Ohio hospital after being injured in a buggy accident. The breaks had been bad and required metal rods to be inserted in both legs. He'd be out of action for a while.

Joe looked around the gloomy living room. The only good thing about being in Stinterton was that Samson was far, far away.

BOREDOM CAUSED Delia Kauffman to wriggle and fidget in her train seat. Looking out the window again, everything was the same as ten minutes before—a barren landscape of nothingness. Sparse trees reached up bare branches among the grass that was parched from months of scarce rainfall.

If Delia had still believed in signs, the scenery alone would've been a foreboding one, saying, 'Go home, girl, go home.'

Maybe she'd get a surprise and Stinterton would be a beautiful and picturesque town and nothing like the arid land the train was powering through.

She had to hope the town she aimed to make her long-term home was a nice place. Sometimes, all she had was hope.

All she knew about the town where her Uncle Thomas and Aunt Sylvia lived was that they were trying to attract more Amish families and that was why they were looking for a schoolteacher. The more established a town was, the more likely people—families—would come to stay.

Bishop Luke had told her there were now five families in the community. A woman was temporarily standing in as schoolteacher but with four children and soon expecting her fifth, she wouldn't be able to manage the job for long.

Trying to avoid the smiles from a man across the carriage, Delia looked out the window again, regretting not bringing a book or some knitting to while away the time. Then she closed her eyes and put her head back pretending to be asleep so the man wouldn't bother her. She couldn't work out if he was smiling at her because she was attractive or because he wanted to strike up a conversation about her Amish lifestyle. She never got much attention from men, so she guessed it was the latter. It so often happened when she went somewhere alone.

When Bishop Luke had contacted her father to see if he knew of a young woman willing to move to his small community to teach, Delia knew it was her answer to prayer. The call had come after two weeks of praying for *Gott* to send her a man. That was why she knew she'd meet someone special in Stinterton.

She had a perfect picture in her mind of the kind of man she wanted. Two years ago, she'd written a list describing her future husband's traits. To make sure she wasn't tempted by some lesser man, she'd carried that list everywhere. So far, no man matched her list, but she summoned all her faith to believe this train was bringing her to him.

Now, reality sank in and her faith was tested. How would she find a man in an isolated community which consisted of five families with young children? Even though she only needed one man, it was unlikely she'd find a single one in Stinterton. Her heart craved to be loved, and she had plenty of love to give in return.

Delia reached down and pulled her water bottle out of her knapsack and took a mouthful. Her fussing mother had made sure she had plenty to eat and drink on the train. As much as she'd miss her folks, she had to get away from them if she was ever going to feel grown up. Sometimes they treated her like a five-year-old.

Her thoughts returned to the reason she had taken the

job so far from home. She had to make a change in the hopes of finding her man.

Perhaps there would be a relative of one of these families, a single cousin or brother, who would come for a visit.

Yes, a visitor. That wasn't out of the question. They'd meet and fall in love.

She pushed her water bottle back into her knapsack and then was sure the man was still staring at her. She glanced at him and he gave her a beaming smile and she looked away. The last thing she needed was attention, any kind, from an *Englisher*—an outsider. She was too tired to make small talk or worse, talk about her community and her beliefs and get into an inevitable argument.

She looked out the window again, hoping the man wouldn't move to the unoccupied seat beside her and start talking.

"Now arriving at Stinterton Station," the voice over the loudspeaker boomed. "Passengers for Stinterton, prepare to disembark."

At last!

She grabbed her knapsack and then reached up for her suitcase that was perched at the back of the overhead shelf. The man across the way flew to his feet and retrieved the heavy suitcase for her.

"Thank you." Now she felt mean for her unkind thoughts. She smiled at him and hoped that would make up for it.

"It was no trouble." When he sank back into his seat, she was pleased he wasn't getting off at the same station.

She waited at the doors and when the train stopped,

they opened automatically. Carefully hugging her knapsack and clutching the suitcase containing all her possessions, she stepped down onto the platform.

Looking left and right, all she saw was a middle-aged couple. They were *Englishers,* so they hadn't come for her. Where was the person meant to pick her up?

The engineer blew the whistle and the train doors closed. She stood back and watched the train move away from the station.

Now she was alone.

No one had come for her.

Her heart beat hard against her ribcage as she wondered what to do, and who to call.

Was there a public phone anywhere about?

Bishop Luke would've met her, but now he was in a hospital somewhere in Ohio.

What if they'd forgotten she was coming?

She pulled her heavy suitcase over to a bench and sat down holding back tears. It had been a long and tiresome journey and all the way she'd been wrestling with a mix of dark and doubtful thoughts versus bright and faith-filled ones about the move she was making.

Minutes later, she saw a horse and buggy approaching.

When a man and a woman got out, she recognized Amy, her cousin, and she'd never been more relieved. And, who was the tall and broad-shouldered man with her?

Delia stood up, blinked hard and squinted to get a better view. It definitely wasn't Uncle Thomas. Could this man be the one?

Please don't be married, she thought. The closer the man got, the more his hazy form merged into a familiar figure.

"It can't be," she said under her breath.

When they got even closer, she saw that it was indeed Joe Bontrager, a man she had once known quite well. Part of coming to Stinterton was to have a fresh start. Joe was not part of her new life. He belonged in her past.

This was awful. She'd rather talk to that man on the train than Joe, but she'd have to speak to him. There was no way around it.

She adjusted her prayer *kapp*, tying the strings underneath her chin so the breeze wouldn't blow it away.

Delia licked her lips, wishing she had checked her appearance in the reflection of one of the train's windows. It was too late now to do anything about it.

At least she was wearing her Sunday best, a dark-cherry-colored dress with white apron and *kapp*. But would she have dark circles under her eyes from tiredness and from general dehydration from the train's air conditioning? She prayed he wouldn't notice all of her physical faults and only see the good points, so he'd see she'd grown into a pleasant-looking woman.

She fixed a smile on her face and lifted her chin high, determined for Joe to see a happy and confident Delia.

One thing she couldn't work out was, what was Joe doing here, in Stinterton. And, the next question was, what was he doing with her cousin?

≈

JOE WALKED toward the lone woman on the station. She was the only woman there and she was staring at them, so she had to be Dee. As they drew closer, he couldn't help noticing she was a young woman, not too fat and not too thin.

"There's Dee. She's not brought much with her it seems," Amy said as they walked toward her.

"Just the one suitcase. Unless she's got more somewhere that we can't see." Then the woman's face came into sharper focus. "I think I know her."

"That's right—I didn't think of it before. Dee grew up in the same community as you. It was silly of me not to realize it."

"Dee… Delia." Somewhere in the back of his mind it clicked that Dee was short for Delia.

"That's right, her proper name is Delia. Everyone in the family calls her Dee." Amy left him and hurried to Delia and threw her arms around her.

Delia hugged her back. They hadn't seen each other for three years. When the cousins parted their embrace, Delia looked up into the eyes of Joe Bontrager.

"Hello, Delia."

This was awkward. "Hello, Joe. I didn't know you'd be here. I had no idea. Probably because no one bothered to mention you live here now." She grabbed his hand and gave it a firm shake, and then released it just as quickly.

"I don't—"

She didn't give him a chance to finish what he was going to say. "You're late. It would've been nice if I'd had someone waiting for me when I stepped off the train, but no, there was no one. I didn't time how long I've been waiting. It's been some time and I didn't know if anyone would show up at all."

"I'm sorry, Dee," Amy began. "It was totally my fault. I asked Joe if I could come too and then I couldn't find my coat anywhere. In the end, I found it in the buggy where I'd left it. *Mamm* refused to let me go without it, she said I'd catch my death of cold."

Nervousness caused Delia's mouth to open and she couldn't believe what came out next. "Are you two dating?"

Amy laughed and then Joe said, "No, we just met yesterday. I've only just arrived here myself. I'll get your bag." He grabbed her suitcase while she threw the knapsack over her shoulder. Joe continued, "Buggy's this way."

"I just thought with the two of you coming to get me like this I assumed you were. You say you've just met?"

Amy looped her arm through Delia's as they walked to the horse and buggy. "Joe arrived yesterday. He's here looking after things for his uncle, who's Bishop Luke. He went somewhere for a wedding and managed to get into an accident and break both his legs."

"I heard about the bishop's accident. You don't live here, Joe?"

"No. I—"

Delia interrupted him once again. "That's awful, about Bishop Luke. I heard of his injuries, but my father made contact with him and he insisted I still come here. He said someone would be here to meet me. I won't tell him you were late, Joe."

"Err, please don't."

"No, don't, because that wouldn't be fair seeing it was my fault," Amy said.

"I know, you said it was your fault, but it doesn't change the fact that I got off the train and no one was here. How do you think I felt after traveling all this way? I thought I'd been forgotten and no one was coming. I was thinking about looking for a phone, but who would I have called?"

"We knew you were coming though, Dee."

Delia fixed her hands on her hips and glared at her cousin.

Amy hung her head. "I'm sorry, Dee."

"It's fine. I've already forgiven both of you. And by both, I mean you too, Joe, even though you haven't apologized."

"That's good of you," Joe said, in a tone that was disturbingly unemotional.

"The bishop also said the children shouldn't be disadvantaged because of his accident. Bishop Luke is your uncle, Joe, is that right?"

"That's correct. Uncle Luke and my Aunt Mary are staying in Ohio until he's better. I said I'd look after things here. They hope to only be a few more days, just as soon as he can travel."

Delia shook her head. "It might be a while with two broken legs. Even if he went in a wheel chair, wouldn't it be hard for your aunt to push him in and out of the train and everywhere else?"

Joe shrugged his shoulders. "I'm just saying what they said. I'm willing to stay however long it takes."

"Okay, good to know." Delia offered him a smile and

he looked away, just the same as she'd looked away from the man in the train just a short time ago. She knew Joe had no interest in her. Had God brought her all this way for Joe to break her heart all over again?

"I haven't seen you for so long, Dee," Amy said.

"I know. I've been trying to count up the years. Would it be three?"

"About that."

"You've been here before, Delia?" Joe asked.

"No, never. Amy and her family came to visit us. The last time they came for a wedding, I think."

"That's right. I can't remember whose wedding it was. It was some years ago now."

"I just thought of something. Your uncle was in Ohio for a wedding and got into that accident." Delia laughed. "Joe, do you think weddings are dangerous? Is that why you've never married?" As soon as she said it, she realized how ridiculous it sounded. It wasn't even funny. She looked at Amy, who gave a weak laugh in support.

Joe shook his head. "No, I've never married for an entirely different reason and that's a subject for another day."

"How long do you plan to be here for, Joe?" Delia asked before she realized they'd just discussed that.

"I'm not too sure at the moment." He put her case in the back of the buggy.

Delia put her hand out. "Careful with that. There are breakables in there."

"I'm sorry."

She laughed to lighten the mood. "Sorry. I'm sure nothing's broken. I wrapped them well."

11

Amy touched Dee lightly on her arm. "Why don't you sit in the front, Dee?"

"Thank you, I will." Delia took a deep breath, hitched up her long dress and climbed into the front of the buggy. A minute later, Joe got into the buggy beside her.

She'd always imagined how wonderful it would be to sit next to Joe in a buggy. In her mind, though, it had been a different scenario than the current reality. In some of her daydreams, they'd been courting and in other daydreams, the back of their buggy was full of their children while she carried a young babe in her arms.

When they went over a bump, she bounced back to reality.

Joe'd had plenty of time to change his mind about her and he clearly hadn't. She had to forget him and look for the man God had for her—the man who matched everything on her list.

If God was faithful, He would hear her prayers and this man would be waiting for her somewhere in Stinterton. She believed it with all her heart.

CHAPTER TWO

*J*oe was embarrassed seeing Delia after so many years. Things hadn't ended well between them, and it was a blessing that her family had moved away not long after. It had saved the awkwardness of bumping into her time and again.

She looked the same, with the light-colored wispy spirals of hair that still managed to escape her prayer *kapp* to frame her oval face. Her skin was just as creamy smooth, and he loved her adorable dimples, one in each cheek. Somehow, he always found people with dimples were happy, friendly, and approachable. The thing was, her personality had never matched her delicate appearance.

She was far too loud, and all her non-stop talking had irritated him now just as it had back then.

Things only got worse the closer they got to Amy's house.

From the start of the ride, Amy had remained quiet while Delia spoke volumes about everything in sight: from the clouds and trees to the strange smells of the outer town limits. She even risked offending Amy by saying the town should be called Stinky Town not Stinterton. Then she laughed about it while Amy didn't comment.

He was soon to find out that nothing was beyond measure for Delia when it came to talking. After a time, he couldn't decide if Delia was seeing how long she could speak before someone else would get a word in.

She was annoyingly loud, but he wondered if he sensed a certain vulnerability in amongst all that chatter.

"Are we going straight to your house, Amy?" asked Delia.

Finally, she had asked a question, which meant she was allowing someone else to speak.

"It's up to Joe."

Delia turned to face Joe. "I'm not tired at all. I should be, but I'm not. I slept a lot on the train, while holding onto my bag with all my money. Actually, I sat on it." Delia laughed. "Otherwise all my money might've been stolen. I brought all my savings with me. Once I get a permanent place, I'll buy a horse and buggy since I'm never moving from here. What do you think about that, Joe?"

Joe struggled to remember the original question. He asked a question of his own and hoped he wouldn't be caught out for not listening. "I guess I could show you the schoolhouse now if you want to see that."

"I'd love to. That would be simply *wunderbaar.*"

"Okay." He spoke quickly while he could. "The schoolhouse is also where we hold the meetings. With everyone living in a radius of Bishop Luke's house and the town, it

14

was a practical decision to have a central meeting point. Everyone agreed to it, so my uncle, with the community's help, built a huge meeting house. It's too large for the current population of the small community, but they have faith it will grow."

Delia pushed some stray hairs back into her *kapp*. "Excuse me? I don't understand. Did you say a meeting house? I've never heard of such a thing."

"Yes."

Amy explained, "Rather than meet in our homes on the scheduled Sundays, we meet there, and that doubles as the schoolhouse too. Other communities have designated a meeting house, we're not the first. Maybe we're the first having it double as a schoolhouse, I'm not sure about that."

"I didn't know that I wouldn't have a separate schoolhouse. No one told me about that. It doesn't seem convenient."

He glanced over at Delia. "You do have one. Just not on Sundays or whenever they want to hold a meeting or an event. It's not a problem, is it?"

"I guess not. No, it's not but, we'll have to pack everything away every Friday afternoon. I'll have the children help."

"That's what Eleanor's been doing," Amy said. "It hasn't been a problem for her. Eleanor's the lady who's been the teacher while Bishop Luke's been looking for a permanent teacher. Now she's only weeks away from giving birth to her fifth baby."

"I know. Bishop Luke told me that. That's why he said I should come without delay. I think God wants me here for a reason. I will be sure to thank Eleanor when I meet her. I'm hoping she'll tell me some things about each child that will be useful to know. It would be convenient to know which ones I can rely on and which ones are daydreamers."

Amy leaned over to the front. "You do realize that Bishop Luke's house is on the same property as the schoolhouse?"

"Oh? What other surprises are waiting for me?" Delia laughed so loudly it hurt Joe's ears.

"I'm not sure what you've been told and what you haven't." He pulled on the reins, stopping the horse and buggy in front of a large store. "Here we are. The general store is on our left and that blue house to the right is my Uncle Luke's."

"Bishop Luke," Amy corrected.

Delia raised herself up. "Why are we stopping here? Where's the schoolhouse?"

Joe said, "I'm just showing it to you. So you get a feel for where everything is. The big building behind his house is the meeting house."

"Oh. I see it. I didn't expect it to be so large. I thought that was another house."

Joe moved the horse and buggy onward, turning into the driveway and then finally, he stopped the buggy at the house.

"I didn't expect it to be so big," Delia said, as they all got out of the buggy. "It's large, that's for sure." Her eyes were fixed on her new schoolhouse.

"I'll show you." They followed Joe as he led the way.

He flung the door open and both women stepped inside. "What do you think, Delia?"

She looked around at the spaciousness. At the far end was a large blackboard in front of five rows of small wooden desks and chairs. The rest of the room was an empty void. "This is nice. So lovely. I can't wait to meet all the children and start the lessons. Oh, the place is so empty my voice is echoing. Do you hear that?" She put her hand up to her ear. "Echo, echo, echo."

"I hear it," said Amy.

"Maybe some rugs on the floor will take that noise away if it bothers you," Joe suggested.

"It doesn't upset me. Not much bothers me except for being abandoned at a train station." She walked forward until she reached the desks, and bent down and ran her fingers over the top of the front desk. Then she stood in front of the blackboard and turned around. She took hold of a ruler and rapped it on the desk a couple of times until she got Joe and Amy's attention. "Good morning, everyone. Please take your seats." She giggled noisily.

Amy laughed and joined in, sitting on a tiny chair behind one of the small desks. "Come on, Joe, play along," Amy urged.

He took a deep breath. He didn't have time for silly children's games. Even when he was younger he had never enjoyed them. "No, the chairs wouldn't hold my weight. I'll pass."

Delia continued, "Everyone take out your books."

Amy laughed. "Sit, Joe. You must."

He chuckled. "I'm fine."

17

"Oh, spoilsport. It's no fun if we don't all play." Amy pouted.

"Joe doesn't like to have fun. That's clear enough."

He folded his arms in front of him. "That's right. I don't."

"What do you do for fun, Joe?" Delia asked, walking over to him.

He took his hat off and rubbed his head. "Not much."

"Hmm, I was right. It was just as I thought." She jabbed a finger through the air pointing at him. "You don't remember how to have fun. No one should lose the child inside them. It makes life far too dull."

Amy swiveled in the small chair to look at Joe. "You must like to do something."

He thought hard. "I used to like harness racing when I was younger."

"I don't remember you ever doing that," Delia snapped.

"No one knows everything about me."

Delia frowned wondering what he meant. Did he have secrets?

"Why did you leave it off?" Amy asked.

"I had an accident and hurt my leg."

Delia looked down at his leg. "You're walking well. I'd say you lost your nerve, didn't you?"

He frowned at Delia and wished he hadn't suggested bringing her to the schoolhouse. It would've been easier to take her straight to the Hostetlers and leave her there. "If that's what you want to believe, then you can believe it."

She fixed her hands on her hip and stared at him intently. "What else do you do with your time?"

He wasn't going to provide anymore bullets for her to shoot at him. He turned it back onto her. "Forget about me. What do you do?"

She looked up at the ceiling. "I like to take long walks. I like picnics, too, and I like gardening. It's rewarding planting seeds, waiting and then watching the green shoots peep above the soil. I love watching things grow."

"Interesting. What about you, Amy?" he asked.

"I guess I like sewing and doing things with *Mamm*, like baking and things like that. We bake a lot on Saturday. We call Saturday our baking day. You'll be able to help us now that you're here, Dee. It'll be so much fun."

"I will. I'd love doing things like that with you all until I get a place of my own."

"Oh, I thought you'd stay with us forever, Dee."

"No. I never said that. I told you just now I plan to get somewhere as soon as I can."

"That might be a problem," Amy said.

"Why? Are your parents going to lock me up and throw away the key, keep me a prisoner and only let me out on weekdays to teach school?"

Amy giggled. "No, don't be childish. The reality of this town is that there aren't that many places around where you could stay. You'll be comfortable with us. It's been lonely since my older sisters left, and I'd like you to stay."

"I'm not worried about whatever reality you or anyone else believes. I believe in my own reality. I believe something in faith and then I believe it will work out."

Joe smiled at her words. At least she wasn't wishy-washy. She was a woman with an opinion and he admired her determination.

"Don't worry, Amy, I'll have to talk to your parents as soon as I can. I hope I didn't give them the wrong impression. I'm so excited to finally live on my own and have my own place."

"But, Delia, if there's nowhere, then there's nowhere, it doesn't matter who believes what. You don't know yet how small this town is. I mean, it's not small in one way, it's kind of all spread out with farms. We have no small houses, like you would have in the suburbs where you come from. The only place you'll find to stay is a bedroom with another family in our community, so you might as well just stay with us."

Amy's words were starting to put a dent in Delia's faith. "I'll see the town tomorrow and see for myself."

Joe said, "I hate to tell you this, Delia, but you've just seen the town."

She narrowed her eyes at him. "What do you mean?"

"The store is all there is. It's like a one-stop-shop for everything anyone needs, and then there is the house next to that, which is actually a café."

"That's it? There's nothing else?"

"Nothing."

Delia bit her lip. She used to love visiting the farmer's markets and going to horse auctions, even window shopping at the stores, but now she'd never be able to do any of that again. Not until the town grew and that could take many years. What if it never grew? "It can't be possible. I mean, I thought there'd be more here even though there are less people."

"That's it," said Amy. "We grow everything we need and trade things between ourselves. Then if the store doesn't carry whatever else we need, they order it."

"I see. That all makes sense. I will get my own place somehow, in some way. Don't you worry about that." She reminded herself that God had sent her there for a reason. He'd work things out. She was positive God would want her to be happy and she didn't want to exchange living at her parents' house only to live permanently with her aunt and uncle. What was the good of that? Besides, once she met the man God had for her, she did not want him to court her with her aunt and uncle looking over her shoulder. A place of her own before she moved to her husband's home was vital.

"You could get something if you're rich enough to buy your own house, Dee. Maybe you could buy land and have something built."

"Not yet I can't. I only have enough to get a horse and buggy, and a little left over. One step at a time my *Mamm* always says. I'll have a talk with your parents soon, Amy." Both young women looked at Joe.

"Well," Joe said, "best I get you there now so you can have that conversation."

"Thanks for showing me the schoolhouse. It's much larger and so much better than I expected. I thought it would be a small building. I know I'll be happy here. This is where I'll spend most of my time." Delia spun in a circle with her arms outstretched, shaking off her previous thoughts of doom. "I just love being a schoolteacher and being around children all day. I can't wait to meet each and every one of them." Her dream was to have her own children someday, lots of them. Delia suddenly stopped spinning. "Joe!"

She spoke so loudly, it caused him to jump. "What is it?"

"I can't have you waste all your time. I reckon you'd thought you'd be collecting me and taking me to Amy's, and now I've taken up nearly your whole day."

He frowned at her outburst. She'd sounded so dramatic he thought she must've left half her luggage on the train, or that something else awful had happened. "I just said I'll take you there now."

"Good." Delia took another look around, and repeated, "I know I'll like it here."

As Joe adjusted his hat and headed to the door, he wondered if Delia was trying to talk herself into liking it. "Ready when you are."

While they were walking up to the buggy, a black and white cat came out meowing at them. "Hello, Kitty." Delia knelt down to pat her. "She's got beautiful green eyes. Look at them. They're pretty, like green crystals."

"That's the bishop's cat. Looks like she's about to give birth," Amy said.

"Oh, Kitty, you are too. Where will you have your kitties?" She looked up at Joe and waited for him to say something.

"I've noticed she usually hangs around the barn," Joe said.

Delia stood up. "What you have to do is make sure she has somewhere nice. They like to feel safe and protected."

"It's a cat. They've been having kittens without help for thousands of years. She can find her own place."

Delia frowned at him. "That's not good enough. I'm going to make a nice place for her. Do you have burlap sacks, Joe?"

"I'm guessing there'll be some in the barn."

"Let's go." Delia hurried to the barn and the cat followed.

While Amy and Joe and the cat looked on, Delia proceeded to make a cave-like place in the corner of the barn. She looked back at the others. "What do you think?"

"Looks like a cave," Joe said.

"She should feel safe there," Amy added.

"Come here, kitty kitty. I will call you Kitty because no one seems to know your name."

The cat meowed and walked over. Delia carefully picked her up and placed her in the cave. The cat left immediately.

"She hates it," Joe said.

Delia narrowed her eyes at him. "She'll get used to it. It might be because we're here."

"There's a solution for that. Let's go." Joe walked out of the barn and headed to the buggy followed by Amy.

Delia patted the cat for a moment saying nice things before she joined the others.

WHEN THEY GOT TO THE HOSTETLERS' property, Joe stopped right outside the front door to make it easier to unload Delia's heavy case. Before doing anything, he walked the girls to the house.

The front door slowly opened and Amy's parents,

Sylvia and Thomas, appeared. They welcomed Delia and ushered her into the house.

For Joe, it was another bishop-like duty done, or it would be once he got the luggage inside. She'd left her knapsack on the floor of the buggy, so he grabbed that along with the suitcase.

He set the luggage down just inside the door, making sure he did so carefully so Delia would not reprimand him again.

Delia left her hosts for a moment and walked over to him. "Thank you, Joe. That case is heavy, you must have some muscles."

He managed a smile.

"They're so nice and welcoming," Delia whispered to him. "I'm glad because I don't know how long I'll have to stay here until I find a place of my own."

"Will you stay for a meal, Joe?" Sylvia asked.

"Please stay," Thomas said. "We're about to eat, if you'd like to join us for food and fellowship."

"I wish I could, but I have some things back at my uncle's cottage that require my attention and I'll need some daylight left to do them. Perhaps another day?"

"Of course," Thomas said.

He looked down at Delia's things. "Shall I put these in a bedroom?"

"Aw..." Delia swiped a hand through the air. "I can move them into the bedroom. If you must go, you must." Delia laughed loudly. "I'll see you later then, Joe, I guess."

"Yes, you will. Bye, everyone."

Sylvia walked Joe to the door. "Are you sure you won't stay?"

"It's tempting, but I don't want to fall behind in my duties." He smiled and then headed back outside.

On his way to the buggy, he regretted his decision not to stay for a meal. In front of him was an evening of loneliness, but being a bachelor of thirty-years-old, he was no stranger to that.

He climbed into the buggy and moved the horse forward. When he was at the end of the street, he saw Mike driving toward him in his pickup truck. Mike and his parents owned the general store in town. He'd met Mike the previous day and they had immediately gotten along, even though Mike was an *Englisher*.

Mike slowed his car and then stopped beside the buggy.

"Joe? What are you doing out here?"

"I could ask the same of you." Joe leaned his head out of the buggy with his arm along the window.

"Me? I had to make a delivery. I saw you in front of my store parading two young women around in your buggy. Good for you." He laughed and Joe laughed along with him before he cleared his throat, remembering he was here as a replacement bishop.

"There's a new woman in our community. It was my duty to collect her from the station."

"Well, I guess that stuff comes with being the stand-in bishop, eh? Helping folks and all."

"I suppose so. One of the ladies was Amy, who you know, the other is Amy's cousin, Delia."

Mike raised his eyebrows. "Delia, eh?"

"That's right. She's the new schoolteacher. I've been

tasked with helping her settle in until she starts her teacher duties one week after Christmas."

"That's not too far off."

"I know."

"So, where's Delia staying?"

"With Amy's family."

"Ah."

Joe narrowed his eyes at Mike when he saw a strange look come over his face. Normally he wouldn't be rude enough to ask what was wrong, but somehow he felt it was okay to ask. "What's on your mind?"

Mike shook his head. "Actually, it's Amy who's on my mind. I shouldn't tell you, but she often is."

Joe pushed back his hat. It was odd that a man he'd only met the day before was taking him into his confidence with such information. It wasn't welcome news that an *Englisher* liked one of the women in the community, especially when the bishop was away and he was temporarily overseeing the flock. What would Uncle Luke do, or say? "You know nothing can happen between the two of you, don't you?"

Mike had a faraway look in his eyes. "I've always had the belief that nothing is impossible. This is a free country, the land of opportunity and all, so I like to believe we can make it work."

Joe was unsure whether Amy felt the same about Mike. This could end up being a problem. "The thing is, she's Amish and we don't—"

"Yeah, I know. But, what if I join up?"

Something made Joe laugh, and then he stopped. He didn't want Mike to think he was laughing *at* him.

"There's a lot in it. It's not as simple as that. It's not like buying a ticket to a baseball game."

"I didn't think it would be easy, but she's worth it. I'd change my life for her in a heartbeat."

He sensed Mike's longing and desperation. "Does she know how you feel?"

Mike hesitated a moment and then shook his head. "Nah. I've felt this way for years. If she knows anything, she doesn't know the full extent of my feelings."

Joe was tempted to tell Mike to forget it. Forget his interest in Amy, and forget about joining their community. Someone with as much passion as he had would not forget something so easily. This needed to be handled carefully and with prayer. "We can talk further about it later if you want."

A smile spread across Mike's face. "Yeah, why not? I should get back to making deliveries. I have a few more stops to make before I can call it a day. We'll get together soon then, eh? Maybe meet up for a feed and talk about what I just mentioned?"

"Sure."

Mike grinned. "Really?"

"Yes."

"Okay, then. Come into the store whenever you can. I'll treat you to lunch at the café any day this week. You'll find me at the store."

"Thank you. I'd like that. See you later, Mike."

Mike held his hand in the air while he accelerated away, leaving the horse and buggy in a cloud of Stinterton dust.

Joe coughed and waved a hand in front of his face.

He'd have to get used to the dust, or pray for snow to hurry and cover the ground. It would be a welcome relief. He moved his horse forward, hoping he could help Mike. Then it wasn't long before his thoughts turned to Delia.

He tried to remember why they'd only ever gone out for two buggy rides when they were younger. He'd been attracted to her as soon as he was old enough to take a girl out in his buggy alone, but then things went dreadfully wrong between them. She didn't seem as loud back then, but she'd immediately thought they were on the road to marriage after their second date. He had no such plans. In the back of his mind he had figured he'd marry in his mid to late twenties, but he had never been one for sticking to schedules or plans. That was why he was thirty and single.

Now, meeting her again this many years later, he was glad he'd made that choice. She was the total opposite from the kind of woman that would suit him.

CHAPTER THREE

On day three of his visit to Stinterton, Joe washed up after his morning breakfast and then decided to clean his hosts' house from top to bottom. The house had been vacant for three weeks before Joe got there and he couldn't help noticing the fine layer of dust that covered everything. Prior to his cleaning spree, the daily duties of horse care loomed large, so he headed outside to muck out the stable and feed his uncle's horses. Thomas, being the community's closest man to the bishop's house, had been looking after them over the last few weeks.

His uncle had three horses, all of them dark bays with differing markings. One had no face markings and two white front socks, one had a star on his face and the other had a blaze. He'd have to ask Amy if she knew their names.

Neither his Uncle Luke nor Thomas had given him any particular instructions about them, so he walked to the stable to check them to see how they were doing.

After inspecting all three he found they had recently been shod and they all seemed sound.

He opened the gate and the horses slowly sauntered out of their stalls, swishing their tails and nudging each other with their noses. Joe saw and smelled from the bedding in their stalls it hadn't been changed for some time. He had a fair bit of work ahead of him today. Thankfully, the barn was well stocked with straw bales.

When he followed the horses into the circular yard, he looked up into the gray sky and saw dark clouds in the distance. Rain was coming.

He pulled up his sleeves and got to work. Two and a half hours later, with the cat watching him all the while, he was just putting the last layer of clean straw down in the last of the stalls when he heard a horse and buggy.

With pitchfork in hand, he walked outside to see Amy driving the buggy with Delia next to her. He set the pitchfork against the wall and dusted off his hands. "Good timing," he muttered as he walked toward them.

He noticed they looked at him and they both laughed as though they were sharing a secret joke. Were they laughing at him?

He tipped his hat back on his head as they both stepped down from the buggy. "Good morning," he called out.

"Good morning, Joe," Amy said.

"Hi, Joe."

"What brings you out here?" he asked.

"Out here? You're in the middle of town, silly," Delia said. "Although it is a little weird that there's only one store and one café and they call it a town."

He'd only been with Delia for less than one minute and she was already getting on his nerves. No one had ever called him silly. It seemed a strange comment, but he was determined to look past it. Uncle Luke would come into contact with all kinds of people, Joe reminded himself, so he made an effort.

Amy said, "We don't need a lot of shops out here. Anything we need, Mike orders in for us."

"You've said that already. I'm sure I'll get used to it here, grow to love it, even."

Amy smiled. "You will." Then Amy looked at Joe. "We came here to see if you'd like to come to dinner tonight. We'd really like you to join us."

He took off his hat and scratched his head, looking for a reasonable excuse. He'd never been one for too much socializing. When he became aware that the two girls were scrutinizing his silence, he looked up. "I'd be delighted."

"Excellent," Amy said. "*Mamm* told me not to take no for an answer. She said I had to talk you into it."

"And she didn't need to," Delia said.

"What time would you like me there?"

"Shall we say six o'clock?" Amy asked.

"Or just come any time you feel like it," Delia said, adding her raucous laughter that was becoming a trademark.

"Six will be fine. I'll look forward to it. And, which of you ladies is cooking?"

They looked at one another. "It'll probably be a joint effort," Amy said. "With my mother cooking as well."

"I'll look forward to it."

31

"Yes, you already said that." Delia stared at him.

"Thank you for asking."

"It's the least we can do since you came all this way to help out Bishop Luke," Amy said. "No one else stepped up to take his place."

"What were you doing just now with that pitchfork?" Delia asked.

"I was mucking out the horses' stalls."

"That reminds me, I'll need to get a horse soon."

"Do you?" he asked.

"Yes, but I suppose I need a place to live first so I've got somewhere to keep the horse."

"I'll do what I can to help you find a place," Joe said.

Delia's eyebrows rose. "Would you?"

"Yes."

"Thank you. It'll just be me, so I just need a small place without much yard unless it's easy to maintain. I'll need a barn, too, for the buggy and the feed and all that."

"Of course."

"I told you already, Dee, there's nowhere. You'll find that out too, Joe, when you help her look. You'll only be wasting your time."

"You never know, something might turn up unexpectedly. What are you doing today?" Delia asked him.

"I thought I'd clean the house when I finish up out here."

Amy frowned. "No. The ladies in the community will do that for you."

"Nonsense. I'm here to do everything."

"But you shouldn't have to clean the house."

"I don't see why I shouldn't. I'm not going to sit

around and do nothing while women clean for me. It would be different if I had other things I could be doing, but right now I don't."

"But let me just—"

"No, Amy. I want every moment of my time here to be productive. Everyone has busy lives, I'm sure. I'm the one who doesn't have much going on right now."

"If you insist…"

"I do."

While they were talking, another horse and buggy came toward the house.

Amy peered at it. "Ah, this is Mr. and Mrs. King. They're coming to say hello to you, Joe, I'd say. They're your closest neighbor apart from us. They're only two miles to the west."

"Oooh goodie. Do they have children?" Delia asked.

"They do. Twin boys about ten, and a girl around eight."

"I hope they brought them, too."

Joe said, "It looks like they're alone in the buggy."

"Mr. King is the deacon," Amy whispered.

Joe was a little confused. If they had a deacon, why was he there? He'd been told there was no one who could stand in for the bishop. That was why Joe had thought the community was so small, if it only had a bishop and no other oversight.

The three of them waited until the buggy came close to them. Mr. King jumped out and walked forward. "Joe, is it?"

"Yes." Joe offered his hand and Mr. King shook it.

"I'm Jed King and this is my wife Sarah."

Sarah walked over and nodded politely to Joe.

Delia liked the look of them immediately, especially Sarah. She guessed her to be in her forties. She stood next to her husband and seemed very shy.

"So..." Delia stepped forward. "You wouldn't have met the new schoolteacher yet, would you? It's me! I'm Delia Kauffman. Just call me Delia, or Dee. My family calls me Dee. I answer to either." Delia moved closer and shook their hands.

"We're all so happy to have you here. You do have experience, the bishop told us, and that's why we're all so pleased," Mr. King said.

"That's right," Mrs. King agreed.

"Yes, I've been a schoolteacher about five years now. And, Mr. King, you're the deacon, is that right?"

He nodded.

"Then why aren't you..." She looked at Joe and didn't want to put her foot into anything. Mr. King might've refused the job of taking over for the bishop and he could've had any number of reasons for doing so. "Forgive me. I'm way too nosy. People tell me that all the time."

"It's fine. You can ask anything, Delia."

She took a deep breath. "Why did Joe come here if... couldn't you have..."

"You're right, I could've done Bishop Luke's duties while he was gone, but it wasn't the right time." Mr. King looked at his wife as though needing her approval to say what he said.

"That's right. It wasn't the right time," Sarah repeated.

"It's cold out. Why don't we all go into the house? It's much warmer."

"We won't. We should probably go now, thanks anyway, Joe." Amy turned and told the Kings, "Dee's staying at my place."

"We'll see you at the Sunday meeting." Mr. King nodded to Delia.

"Oh, and I can't wait to meet your children, and all the other children too."

Mrs. King smiled. "They're excited to meet you as well."

"All right then. Come on, Dee, we should go back and help *Mamm*."

"We'll see you tonight, Joe," Delia said.

"You will. Thanks for the invitation." As they walked away, and just to annoy Delia, Joe said for a third time, "I'll look forward to it."

Delia glanced back over her shoulder at him and he laughed, then the girls continued to their buggy.

When Joe went inside with Mr. and Mrs. King, Delia grabbed Amy's arm. "Wait a minute. I'm going to look for that cat. Are you sure you don't know her name?" Delia kept moving toward the barn.

"No I don't."

"Kitty it is then."

"Don't be long. *Mamm* is expecting us home."

Delia stopped inside the barn door. "Here kitty, kitty. She's not coming out. She's probably fast asleep in the cave I made for her."

"Let's go," Amy said.

Delia looked in the cave and there was no cat. She looked around the barn and there was no sign of her. After she called a couple of more times and there was still no sign, she called out to Amy, "I'm coming."

Amy was waiting for her just outside the barn. "Couldn't find her?"

"No. I hope she's all right."

"She'll be okay. She's lasted this long."

"I know, but she's about to have babies."

As they climbed into the buggy, Amy said, "You must love cats."

"I do. I wonder if I'll be able to keep one in my new place. That's what I'll believe for. I'll believe I'll be able to keep a cat and it'll happen."

Amy kept silent as she moved her horse and buggy back onto the road.

CHAPTER FOUR

*a*s the girls drove away, Delia looked out the small back window of the buggy.

"Joe's so handsome, don't you think so, Dee?"

"He's all right, I suppose." Delia swiftly faced the front. "You don't *like* him, do you?"

Amy gave her a sidelong glance. "I'm not sure. What do you think of him?"

"Yes, well, he seems nice enough."

"But you know him already, Dee. You grew up with him. You should have more to say about him than that."

"We grew up in the same community, but that doesn't mean we were friends. And I never had much to do with him." That wasn't the whole truth, but Delia was too embarrassed to tell Amy that he'd rejected her. She didn't want to even think about it. "And then my family moved away."

"Bishop Luke wouldn't have asked him here if he didn't trust him. That shows that he's well respected."

"Why didn't anyone volunteer to help out, maybe

someone closer?" asked Delia. "Someone like Mr. King. He is the deacon after all."

"They're all busy with farming and things. I'm not sure, to be honest. Maybe they did offer and Bishop Luke sent Joe anyway."

"Hmm. Or maybe Joe is the only man your bishop could find who didn't have any commitments?"

"I didn't think of that," Amy said.

"Yes that's got to be right, he had no commitments."

"It sounds like you don't think much of him, Dee."

"Oh, I do. He's a very nice man as far as I know. And he comes from a good family."

"That's important."

"Yes, it is." Delia closed her eyes tightly and prayed that her cousin wasn't falling for Joe. She didn't want to be selfish, but it would be painful to watch her cousin find happiness with Joe.

"Do you think he'd make a good husband?" Amy asked.

"I was just thinking that. You read my mind. I think he'd make a great husband and I was wondering why he's never married. Do you know anything about that?"

Amy shook her head. "Do you?"

"I don't, but we moved away from that community when I was about nineteen, remember? I didn't hear much about him or his family after that. First time I saw him, apart from maybe the occasional wedding, was yesterday. He was so skinny back then when I knew him. Tall and skinny. He's still tall, but he's more muscled now."

"You've heard nothing about him, no rumors or anything?" Amy asked.

"That's right, no rumors."

"That is amazing. There's usually talk between the communities. News is shared."

"Well I suppose he had nothing newsworthy going on in his life. He didn't have any babies because he wasn't married and there was no news of him marrying because he wasn't marrying anybody."

"I suppose that's true. I didn't think of that."

Delia fiddled with her *kapp* strings like she always did when she was anxious. "So, are there any men here that you like, or that like you?"

Amy's nose twitched. "Not really."

Not really wasn't a proper answer. It wasn't a yes and it wasn't a no. What was going on with her cousin? She dare not probe further because she didn't want to hear that her cousin was in love with Joe after knowing him for only a day or two. "Joe's not here for long, is he?"

"Not as far as I know. He could stay on when Bishop Luke comes back. I'm not sure what he's planning. I know one thing for sure."

"What's that?" Delia asked, holding her breath.

"Bishop Luke would be delighted if Joe stayed on. It would be another person in the community. He'd find a wife and bring her here and that would make another family."

Delia relaxed a little. "Yes, that's true. He'd need to find a wife from elsewhere because I'm guessing there aren't any single women his age here. Except for the two of us."

They spent the remainder of the journey in silence while Delia tried to decide whether a second chance was possible with Joe or whether God was trying to teach her some kind of lesson. Could He be showing her that Joe was not the man for her, so her heart could forget him once and for all?

AFTER JOE SPENT an hour talking to the Kings, he spent another hour cleaning the house before he realized housecleaning was a never-ending task. When he grew hungry, he remembered his words with Mike about sharing lunch sometime. Today was as good a day as any and he felt like a decent meal rather than a ham sandwich.

He washed his hands, then dried them with a towel while looking out the kitchen window. From there, he had a good view of the store. There were no cars, no delivery trucks and no buggies. It seemed like a quiet time for the store. Joe picked up his hat from where he'd left it on the kitchen table, popped it on his head, then grabbed his black coat and headed out the door while he was pulling it on.

Hopefully Mike would be there and not out doing his deliveries.

Joe shoved his hands in his coat pocket and ducked his head against the chilly wind as he ran across the road.

When he pushed the shop door open, he saw Mike directly in front of him sitting behind the counter.

Mike looked up. "Hello, stranger."

Joe laughed. "Hello again."

Mike closed the book he was writing in. "What can I do for you?"

"I came to have that talk if you're not busy."

"Great timing. I'm due for a break. I'll call my father." He got up and walked through the doorway to the residence where Mike and his parents lived.

Mike was gone for a minute and then he returned. "He's coming. I'm ready."

"Are you sure it's okay?"

"Sure I'm sure. We can have something to eat at the café. Are you hungry?"

"Always."

As they walked to the small house that doubled as a café, Mike asked, "Have you met Pam, the owner of this place, yet?"

"No. This will be my first time here."

Mike made a face. "She's abrupt. Don't take it personally, she's like that with everyone."

"Thanks for the warning."

"Her name's Pam Green."

"Pam Green," Joe repeated. "I'll try to remember that."

They walked through the door and sat down at one of the six empty tables. There was no one else there. As Joe opened the menu, he leaned over and whispered, "Where is everybody?"

"I'm sure someone will come soon being lunchtime and all. There's normally someone else here."

"That's surprising."

"Well, you shouldn't be surprised. We have more people in this town than you'd think."

A minute later, a middle-aged man walked through the door, nodded to Mike and Joe before he took a seat at a table on the far side of the room.

"Morning, Barry," Mike called out.

"I think it's afternoon, Mike."

Mike laughed. "I think you're right. Barry, this is Joe. Joe's taking over temporarily for the Amish bishop."

He nodded to him. "Nice to meet you, Joe."

"Thank you. Likewise."

Barry picked up the menu and then a woman bustled through the internal doorway. She was a heavyset short woman who looked like she didn't know what a smile was. Her size was amplified by her frilly white blouse and a skirt that was far too tight. Her graying hair was pulled back into a ponytail, and her mouth was one straight line, as though someone had drawn it.

Mike was bright and cheerful as he introduced Joe as the Amish bishop's nephew. She raised her heavily pencil-drawn eyebrows slightly and looked him up and down. "So you're replacing the Amish bishop, and you're his nephew?"

"Only temporarily replacing him, and yes I'm his nephew."

She readied her pen and paper. "What'll it be?"

Joe looked down at the menu. "I think I will have the fish and fries and the salad."

She shook her head. "Can't do."

"No?"

"We ain't had no fish for months, and we only have salad in the summer."

"Ah, very well." Joe had another quick look at the menu trying his best not to keep her waiting. "Then I'll have the beef stew with the sourdough bread."

"Can't do. We got no beef this week."

Joe closed the menu. "What do you have?"

"I can do you a hamburger."

"That will be fine."

She looked at Mike. "Two hamburgers, then?"

"Yes, thank you."

She took the menus from them and headed to her other customer.

"Sorry about that, but I tried to warn you." Mike gave a low chuckle.

Joe raised his eyebrows. "I'll know next time."

Mike swallowed hard. "What can you tell me about Amy?"

"Amy?"

"Yes."

"I barely know her."

"Yeah, I know that, but you know how all this works with her being Amish. How do I get to date her?"

Now Joe felt extremely unqualified and equally uncomfortable. He tried to make his answers the same as Uncle Luke's would've been. "Have you talked to her?"

"Of course I have. She comes to the store all the time."

"That's not what I meant. Is she aware of your feelings?"

Mike grimaced. "I don't think so."

"She's totally unaware?"

"I haven't told anybody."

"The best thing you can do is forget about her."

His mouth turned down. "I thought you'd help."

"I'm telling you as a favor, so you won't waste your time. Her world and beliefs will be totally different from yours. She won't be permitted to date you for a start, and anything beyond that would never be permitted either. I'm sorry, Mike, but there's no way anything between the two of you would work."

"There must be a way. What if she leaves?"

Joe opened his mouth in surprise. "If you care about her, how could you want her to leave?"

"I'm sorry, Joe. I didn't want to offend you. I'm just putting some different things out there into the universe. It is an option, isn't it, if that's what she chooses?"

"I don't see her doing that. She wouldn't want to leave her family and her community. She doesn't seem the kind of girl who'd want to leave. I can't see it happening."

"She wouldn't have to go anywhere; she could stay living here. We could both live here after we're married. Or somewhere close by."

Joe was surprised Mike's feelings were that strong for someone who'd only been a customer at his store. "You're thinking a long way ahead."

"I can't help it. She's an attractive woman, but it's more than that. There's something about her that just pulls me towards her. I'm like a moth to a flame."

Joe couldn't help chuckling at Mike's corny words.

"Tell me what I have to do, Joe, and I'll do it. You're the stand-in preacher man."

"Bishop," Joe corrected him.

"Yeah... That. I'm sorry, I'm not trying to be disrespectful."

"You could join the community, but it wouldn't go over well if you were joining for love and love alone. You're supposed to join for spiritual reasons, and your Godly walk."

"My Godly what?"

"Your life… giving up everything for God. You'd be giving up many of the things you're used to."

"Yeah, but gaining the only thing I want."

"You have big plans and big ideas for someone who hasn't told Amy how you feel."

"When you know, you know. You're the only person I've ever told."

"First, you should seek God. See what He wants for you."

"What? See if He wants me to be Amish?"

"Yes. That way you'll be doing things the right way." Joe spent another ten minutes telling him what was involved in joining the Amish community before Pam brought their hamburgers to the table.

Joe stared at the burger that filled the whole plate. It looked like it had been worth the wait. "Thank you. It looks very good."

"Hope it tastes it," Pam said before she turned away.

Joe picked up the burger in both hands and managed to wrap his mouth around it. Mike did the same with his, and conversation ceased while they focused on eating. *Awesome*, thought Joe as he took his last bite.

JOE FINISHED his time with Mike, bought some more groceries and then walked back to Uncle Luke's house. On the way, he thought about Mike's confession, and didn't know how he felt about it. It wasn't every day that an *Englisher* fell in love with an Amish woman, at least it didn't often happen where he was from.

When Joe had first seen Amy a couple of days ago, when she and her parents picked him up from the train station, he had been immediately impressed with her. If he'd been looking for a wife, she would've been the ideal woman. She had a sweet nature and she was polite, as well as being easy on the eyes. He'd decided a long time ago not to marry until he found a woman who fully captured his heart. He'd not marry for the sake of conforming to the expectations of family, or for the sake of convenience.

But, should he stick to what he'd decided years ago? After living on his own for many years, he could see the value in having someone to share his life. Was it unreasonable to expect that someone would be perfect for him when the world itself was imperfect? Every one of his friends was married, and they were happy most of the time. He often felt pangs of envy, seeing them with their wives or playing with their children.

His thoughts returned to Amy. He hardly knew her, but with Mike revealing he was fond of her, she had to be off limits as a potential wife. He wasn't desperately looking for one, but it was never far from his mind either. Maybe Mike would change his life and join them and Joe didn't want anything to stand in Mike's way.

The more he thought about Amy and her potential as a wife, he felt a certain sense of relief. Almost as though he was off the hook and didn't have to explore the possibility of love with Amy.

He never forgot his father's advice that people were a long time married, so they should choose wisely. Besides that, there was something inside him that wanted to be different from others in the community. Now he was older, it was time to fight against that urge. That was why he'd volunteered to help his uncle.

It had never been easy to maintain individuality in the Amish community where losing one's self and thinking of others first was the goal. He'd outwardly showed his rebellion by his short haircut and his non-conforming clothing choices that skated along the edge of acceptability.

Knowing he couldn't remain a rebel forever, he was determined to use his stay in Stinterton to mend his ways, become a proper member of the Amish community, and … maybe even blend in.

CHAPTER FIVE

ust before six o'clock, Joe knocked on the Hostetlers' door. He wasn't as hungry as he could've been because of his huge lunch.

Mrs. Hostetler opened the door and invited him in. She sat him down in the living room with her husband, Thomas, before she hurried back into the kitchen with Amy and Delia.

"They're doing last minute dinner preparations. They like everything just so."

"I thought as much." Joe felt at home with the Hostetlers. As soon as he met them he felt like he'd known them forever.

"Have you heard from Bishop Luke today?" Thomas asked. "Or from Samson?"

"Samson? Is he coming here?" Joe's heart thumped hard. Was his worst nightmare coming true?

Thomas frowned. "Ah, now I think about it. Bishop Luke chose you over him."

"So, he mentioned Samson to you?"

Thomas nodded. "He preferred you to come. So that was that."

Joe slowly let out the breath he was holding onto.

"What about Bishop Luke? Have you heard from him?" Thomas asked.

"I have. I called the hospital just before I came here. He said Mary wants him to stay until the warmer weather even if he leaves the hospital before then. The doctor said he'll only be in another few days if all goes well."

Thomas shook his head. "Must've been some bad breaks."

"They were. I'm happy to stay however long he wants or needs me, and that's what I told him."

Thomas smiled and gave him a nod. "He said you were reliable."

Joe raised his eyebrows. "He did?"

"Yes."

"Does that surprise you?"

Mrs. Hostetler walked out of the kitchen followed by the girls.

Joe twisted to look at them, while saying, "No, it doesn't surprise me."

When the girls laughed at him, Joe got anxious.

He looked back at Thomas after smiling and nodding a 'hello' to the girls. "What I meant to say is, I know I'm reliable and I'm pleased he does too."

"You wouldn't be here if he didn't trust you," Mrs. Hostetler said.

"The meal smells delicious. Is it chicken?" Joe asked.

"Roasted chicken with roasted rosemary vegetables.

Amy loves to grow herbs and dry them, just as much as she loves her needlework."

"I can't wait to try them."

"The meal will only be another ten minutes."

Amy headed back into the kitchen followed by Delia.

"It must be a treat to have your niece here," Joe said, as Sylvia sat next to her husband.

"It is. We told her she could stay on here, but she insists on finding a place of her own. There are no places she can stay, but there's no telling her that. She's a stubborn one. She'll have to find it out for herself if she won't take our word for it."

"There is a room available above Mike's store. I remember seeing the sign when I was there today. I've no idea what it would be like. Do you think that's something she'd be interested in? It would be close to the schoolhouse."

"I don't know," Thomas said. "I think she mentioned she wanted a small house somewhere. I'll ask her."

"Are you talking about me?" Delia walked back into the room and sat down.

"We are," Uncle Thomas said.

"Ask me what?"

"I saw a sign today saying there's a room above the general store available for lease."

"Just one room?" Delia screwed up her nose. "I think I can do better than that. And what about a bathroom and a kitchen?" Delia shuddered. "I wouldn't like to share either of those because I'd feel as though I wasn't really living on my own."

"I'm not too clear on what the sign said. It could be more than just one room."

Delia put her head on the side. "You said you saw a sign?"

"Yes."

Aunt Sylvia said, "It could be the size of an apartment, then, Delia. You should go to see it because there aren't many places around here for lease. It's not like where you come from."

"Thank you. I will take your advice. I'll look at it as soon as I can."

"Would you mind very much taking her to see it tomorrow, Joe?" Thomas asked.

Joe was a little taken aback that they'd ask him. After all, she was staying with them. Perhaps that was something they thought the bishop should do. "I will. How about I pick you up around midday, Delia?"

"I'll be ready and waiting," she bellowed. Her voice was loudly uncomfortable for Joe's ears.

With those lungs she'd make a good schoolteacher. The children at the back of the room would hear her clearly.

"C'mon everyone, dinner is ready," Amy announced from the doorway of the kitchen.

Joe was delighted to have a meal that someone else had cooked. It was a rare treat since he wasn't that good in the kitchen. He'd lived on his own for years and never enjoyed his own cooking but, he often told himself, it had kept him alive so far and he hadn't suffered food poisoning once. He mainly lived on boiled vegetables and ham sandwiches. Best he keep that to himself.

He sat down to a table covered with a red and white

checkered tablecloth. Amy and Delia brought all the food in bowls and placed them in the center of the table. Lastly, an ample sized chicken along with a carving knife, was placed in front of Thomas.

Then the girls sat down and everyone closed their eyes and each said a silent prayer of thanks for the food.

When they finished, Thomas picked up the knife and set about carving the chicken. He looked up at Joe. "You're our guest tonight, Joe, so I'll ask you first. What portion of the bird would you like?"

Joe's mouth watered. "Anything's all right with me."

"You must have a preference." Delia looked at him from under her dark lashes.

"I don't. Each piece is as good as the other."

"I've never heard of anyone not caring. There's so much variety to a chicken. There's dark meat, light meat, and then there's the skin. Wings, legs..."

Delia went on and on, until Joe nearly asked her to stop her persistent chatter. Her constant babbling was hurting his ears. He chuckled to cover his annoyance. "It's fine. I truly don't mind. I'm grateful for anything that's on my plate."

Delia frowned at him while Thomas placed a chicken leg and some of the white meat on a plate and Sylvia took it and passed it to Joe. "Help yourself to everything else," Sylvia told him.

"Thank you, I will. It all looks amazing and I can't wait to try the rosemary vegetables."

Delia shook her head slightly as she looked down at the table while waiting to be passed a plate of chicken.

"How are you liking Stinterton so far?" Joe asked Delia.

"I've barely seen it."

"Joe, you should show her around after you take her to see the apartment," Sylvia suggested.

"Okay. I'm hardly an expert though, since I've only been here a day longer. You should come too, Amy."

"I can't. If I could I would, but I'm doing something else tomorrow."

"That's settled then," Thomas said. "Thank you, Joe."

"You're welcome." Now, he couldn't back out of it. Joe cut a portion of chicken and popped it into his mouth. He wasn't looking forward to tying up his day with Delia when he was trying to sort out his own life. He wouldn't have minded so much if Amy could've gone with them. She would've softened Delia's boisterous manner. "The chicken is delicious."

"Amy looks after the chickens. She killed this one and cooked it."

"Impressive." He nodded, but didn't want that image in his head while he was eating it.

"I had chickens at home when we had the farm, before we moved," Delia said. "They were our pets and we only had them for eggs."

"Yes, but surely when they got old..." Sylvia's voice trailed off.

Delia focused her attention on cutting a piece of chicken. "I can't think about that right now."

"What do you want to think about?" Sylvia asked.

"Christmas. It's my favorite time of year." Delia's face beamed.

"I like it also," Thomas said. "And it's not far away. You'll miss your family, Delia."

"I know, but I'm looking forward to spending Christmas with all of you. You're all my family." She laughed when she looked at Joe. "You're not. I didn't mean you."

"I realise that."

Sylvia tapped Joe on the shoulder. "Joe, you must have Christmas dinner with us. You have to. You haven't met anyone else yet, so ours is the first invitation."

"I'd love that. Thank you."

Thomas set the carving knife down. "We're getting in first because we know you'll have many opportunities to go other places for Christmas."

"My favorite thing about Christmas is the play," Amy said.

Joe looked at her. "What play is that?"

The smile left her face. "Oh, Joe, you don't know about the play?"

He stared at her blankly. "No, should I?"

"Yes, because with Bishop Luke gone, you're in charge of it."

Sylvia put her fork down and covered her mouth. "Oh dear, I thought Bishop Luke would've told you about the play and had you make the arrangements. What will happen if there is no play this year? Everyone will be so upset."

Now he felt even more inadequate. He rubbed his forehead, regretting his decision to help his uncle. What did he know about plays? It was going to end up being an embarrassment. Food caught in his throat and he grabbed the glass in front of him and took a mouthful of water to wash it down. "I'm in charge of… what exactly?"

"The Christmas play. We do one every year," Amy said.

Delia put her fork down and clapped her hands. "I'm used to doing plays for the schoolchildren. At my old school, we did at least two every year. I'd love to help if I could. Could I, Joe?"

For the first time, he was thankful for Delia being there, but could he stand to be around this loud woman any longer than absolutely necessary? He could put earplugs in, but then he mightn't be able to hear anything else and he would have to interact with her. "Would you, Delia?"

"Of course I would. I love organizing things."

That was nice for him to hear because he was someone who struggled with planning. He employed people to do that. Sadly, his personal life was evidence of his dislike of structures, plans, and timelines.

"That's settled then, Joe. Dee will assist you."

"Thank you, Delia. I'm grateful for all the help I can get. And what about you, Amy, will you have time to help? Perhaps you can be a character in the play."

"I'm too shy for that. I find it hard to stand up in front of people and speak."

Delia laughed. "I have no problem with that, Amy. If you can't help, it doesn't matter. I'm sure we'll manage. Maybe we'll give you a part with no talking. Yes, that's what we'll do."

Joe stared at Delia, amazed that she asked and answered her own question without drawing a breath.

Delia tried not to look at Joe so much. It was hard

because he was so handsome with his chiseled features and square, masculine jaw. Now she believed she was getting her second chance. First with him showing her the place above the general store, and then with him allowing her to help him with the play.

Tonight, she wouldn't be able to sleep thinking about all the time she'd be spending with him.

The more she thought about it, the more she realized living above the general store would be a perfect location while Joe was staying at the bishop's house.

CHAPTER SIX

*T*he next morning, Joe couldn't wait for an acceptable time to call his uncle. He had the number of his hospital room.

When the clock on the mantle struck nine, he headed to the phone in the barn.

He had to find out more about this Christmas play. If things went to plan, his uncle would say not to bother with the play this year.

That was what he was hoping.

Just as he was reaching for the phone, he saw the cat peeping her head out of the cave Delia had made for her. It made Joe smile. He picked up the phone's receiver and dialed the number of his uncle's hospital room.

"Hello," Uncle Luke said.

"Hello, it's Joe here."

"Joe Here? I'm sorry, but I don't know anyone by that name." His uncle chuckled. Small things like that amused him.

"You sound like you're getting better," Joe said.

"I am. *Gott* is *gut*. How's it all coming along?"

He was surprised his uncle sounded so chirpy. With God's grace, he'd be back home in no time. "Great except... I didn't know I'd have to put on a Christmas play."

"If that's the only problem you've got while I'm gone you're a blessed man."

That wasn't the response for which Joe was hoping. He tried again, in a slightly different vein. "I'm determined to do a good job for you. It's just that I honestly don't know if I'll do a good job at the play. It was a shock to hear about it and I'm told there is a great expectation for it to be good with so many people from miles around coming to it." There was silence for a moment and Joe waited, hoped, and prayed his uncle would allow him to cancel the play.

"If it's all too much for you, I'll call Samson and have him replace you."

Joe hit his head. Samson? Why did his name keep coming up? He hadn't had to think of his cousin for years and now it seemed he was hearing his name on a daily basis. "No, it's fine. Don't send him. It's not necessary. I'll figure it out."

"The play is a big event. As you already know, everyone comes from miles around. They all look forward to it. It's the one time of the year that the whole outlying community comes together."

"Yes, it makes sense for it to go ahead."

"Listen, it's okay. I don't mind sending Samson along to help out. He was unhappy when he learned I'd allowed you to step into my shoes for a time."

"It's fine. Everything's fine. I'm having a great time and the Hostetler's have been so welcoming."

"They're a good lot of people. You should enjoy yourself while you're there. See if you can find yourself a wife."

Joe chuckled.

"No, Joe. I'm serious. Do it now before you get too old and set in your ways. Unless that's happened already, has it?"

Joe ignored that last question. He was probably already set in his own ways, but wasn't everyone set in their own ways? It seemed an odd thing to say. A person couldn't be set in someone else's ways. "I'll give finding a wife some thought. I'm glad you're improving."

"Ah, they say I'm doing as well as can be expected, but that's not telling me much."

"Don't hurry back. Everything's going well here. The play will be amazing."

"I trust you. It's got to be good to have folk come again next year."

"Good. It will be."

"Don't let me down, Joe. I'll hear about it if you do."

Joe's heart beat hard against his chest. Had he known about the play, he wouldn't have come. One thing was for sure, he didn't want Samson anywhere near him. "I won't let you down. You can trust me. Is there anything else I should know?"

"Like what?"

"I don't know, anything at all?"

"I don't think so. If this is too hard for you—"

"It's not. It's fine. Nothing is too hard. Everything is perfect."

"I hope so."

"Just forget about everything here. It's all under control. You just concentrate on getting better."

"I will. Thanks again, Joe." There was a clunking sound in Joe's ear and then everything went silent.

After blowing out a deep breath, Joe replaced the phone's receiver. He brushed off the image of his competitive cousin, so it wouldn't ruin his day.

JOE PICKED up Delia to show her the space for lease above Mike's store.

"Thanks so much for this, Joe. I know you must be so busy with the meeting tomorrow."

"Not too busy. Your aunt said the women will take over and do everything with the food. The building's already set up for the meeting, so that part is done. Other than that, there's not much to do."

"I wasn't talking about any of that, Joe. I was talking about you writing the sermon."

His breath caught in his throat. Sermon? He thought someone else would do that. One of the elders, perhaps. "Oh, that."

Delia laughed at him. "You hadn't even thought about it, had you?"

"No, well, yes. I mean…"

She shook her head. "You've got some work ahead of you."

"I guess I do. You are right. I assumed one of the

elders would give the sermon, or the deacon or the minister."

"Amy said this is such a small community, that there's only a deacon. They had an elder once, but he moved back to Lancaster County, and no one took his place."

"I guess it's up to me, then."

Delia laughed. "I'd say you're right. Do you want some help?"

He took his eyes off the road and frowned at her. "What kind of help? You know women don't preach."

"No, but I can give you ideas. I've always liked the story about the poor man on the side of the road."

"Um, is that in the Bible?"

"Yes. The man was poor or something and people were mean to him and robbed him and hit him and then the nice man came along and looked after him and fixed his wounds."

Joe smiled. "The Samaritan. I like that one as well. He was an unlikely helper."

"Just like you, Joe."

"Me? Why am I an unlikely helper?"

"You're here for your uncle. I thought… never mind."

"No, go on. Say what's on your mind." He held his breath waiting for her to say she thought Samson would be asked.

"I just thought that the bishop would get someone to replace him who was married. All the bishops I've ever known of have been married."

He was relieved that she didn't say what he thought she'd say. "I'm not a bishop, though. I'm just staying in his place and doing what I can to help. He'll only be another week or so, but for some reason he wanted someone here."

"Probably for the play."

Joe cringed. He didn't even want to think about the play. It was bad enough he now had to write a sermon. Joe stopped the buggy outside the general store. "Here we are."

Delia got out of the buggy and they both continued into the store. Mike looked up, saw them and walked over. "Hi there."

"Mike have you met Delia yet?"

"I haven't." Mike stood up and reached out his hand.

Delia shook it. "Just call me Dee. Everyone does. Everyone except for Joe." She smiled up at Joe.

"Delia is Amy's cousin."

A smile lit Mike's face. "Is that right?"

"Yes. I'm the new schoolteacher."

"We're here to see the room that you're advertising for lease." Joe glanced over at the sign. "Says it's a room upstairs."

"You're both here to see it?"

"Yes," Delia answered.

Mike looked from one to the other, frowning. Then Joe guessed what he thought. "It's for Delia. She's staying with Amy's parents, but she doesn't want to stay there forever. I saw the sign and—"

"Now I get it. I'll show you." He closed the door and turned the sign around to say, Back in 5 mins. Then he grabbed a key from behind the cash register. "There is a separate entrance out back, but we can also go up these stairs." He led the way, then he unlocked the door. "It's been closed up a while."

They found themselves in a large well-lit living area with a small kitchen off to one side.

"The bedroom is through there."

Joe stood back while Delia looked around. He couldn't see why the place wasn't perfect for her. She'd only need one bedroom and it had its own kitchen and its own bathroom. Large windows captured the morning sun and the whole place was far more spacious than he had thought it might be.

"Well, how much is it?"

"It has been vacant for a while. I'm sure we can work something out."

"What do you think of it?" Joe looked over at Delia.

"I think it'll suit me." She walked to the windows and looked out. "I'll be able to see you from here, Joe. Spy on you, even." A loud giggle escaped her lips while she opened the window and then called out, "Hello, Joe!"

Mike looked at Joe as though he was surprised by Delia, and Joe could only smile to cover his embarrassment at her behavior.

She swung back around. "So how much, Mike?"

"I'll talk to my folks and see if we can work something out. Can I let you know on Monday?"

"Sure, but don't let anyone else have it before then, please?"

"I won't."

"You'll be able to find Delia at Amy's house," Joe told Mike.

"Perfect. I'll stop by Monday morning and we can work things out from there."

Delia huffed. "All right. I guess it's only a day or two. It would be ideal if I can move in before I start teaching."

"It shouldn't be a problem. You can move in any time next week."

"I'm pleased to hear it." She turned around and looked at Joe. "What do you think? You haven't said one thing."

"I like it. I like it a lot."

She burst out laughing. "I'll take your word for that. You don't seem enthusiastic at all."

"I am. I think it'll be an excellent place for you to live."

She smiled and then swung back to face Mike. "Only problem is, I'll be getting a horse and buggy. Do you have anywhere here I can keep a horse and a buggy?"

"Yeah. Out the back. We've got acres here with all kinds of stables, sheds and barns. You name it, we've got it. We'll work something out for you."

"That makes it perfect. I'll see you on Monday then, Mike, if I don't see you before."

"Okay."

They headed down the stairs.

When they were back in the buggy, Delia said, "Thanks for finding that for me. I don't know why Amy or her folks didn't mention it."

"Perhaps they didn't notice the sign."

"How could they not? It's so large. That's the first thing I saw when I got here."

"Perhaps when you see something for so long, your mind just bypasses it."

She stared at him, wondering if he was talking about

66

them when they were younger. "That could be what it was."

"Or perhaps they weren't looking for signs because they'd rather you stay with them. They seem so pleased to have you there."

"I know, but now I'm away from my parents, and I really want to survive on my own. If I just go from my folks' home to my aunt and uncle's home, there's really not much difference."

"I can see where you're coming from."

"Good. Now all I need is to buy a horse and buggy."

"Just wait and see if you can agree on a price for your… apartment."

"I don't think that'll be a problem. I'm getting a small wage for being the schoolteacher, aren't I?"

His mouth dropped open and he stared at her. "Didn't you discuss that with my uncle before you got here?"

She burst out laughing and doubled over holding her stomach. When she stopped, she said, "You should see your face. You're so funny."

"So you have got that settled, then?"

"I do."

He looked back at the road, annoyed with her for making him look stupid. "You scared me for a moment."

"I'm sorry." Delia laughed at him. "I couldn't resist it."

He had no idea why she found it so funny.

THAT NIGHT, Delia was pleased that her time with Joe had gone well. It wasn't as awkward as she thought it would be, but she saw her laughing annoyed him and for some reason that made her nervous so she did it all the more.

If nothing more developed between them, she hoped they could be friends.

She was also happy he hadn't mentioned their past.

Best that was forgotten.

CHAPTER SEVEN

*J*oe had woken up at first light on Sunday morning and spent hours going over the sermon he'd written the night before. By the time he'd eaten a quick breakfast, he was confident he knew it so well he wouldn't need to refer to his notes.

When the buggies began arriving, he headed outside to greet everyone.

In time the seats in the meeting hall were filling, causing Joe's stomach to churn. He hoped he'd do a good job for his uncle.

After the Deacon opened the meeting in prayer, Joe stood up, Bible in hand and the two men exchanged places. When Joe looked up at all the people staring at him, he hoped he wouldn't disappoint them. This was the first time he'd be speaking in front of a crowd, except for when he was back in school and had to read in front of the class.

Just as Joe opened his mouth to speak, he noticed a

man leaning against the doorway. It was odd that the man was standing there and not sitting down. When he looked harder, he couldn't believe his eyes.

Samson!

It was his cousin staring at him with his arms crossed, looking none too happy.

Everything Joe was about to say left his mind completely. His cousin would love it if he failed, got choked up and couldn't talk.

Joe cleared his throat, choosing to ignore his adversary. "For those of you who don't know me yet, I'm Bishop Luke's nephew, Joe Bontrager. I'll be here staying at his house until he gets back if any of you need anything. I mean to say, let me know if you need anything. That's where I'll be if you need me." He cleared his throat. "Bishop Luke will be back as soon as he's well enough to travel."

He heard murmurs of agreement in the crowd. He looked at the sea of faces and saw only smiles. That made him feel better.

After a deep breath, Joe looked at his cousin who was still standing in the doorway. "Please come in and take a seat," Joe said, since he knew his cousin wouldn't have expected him to directly address him.

Everyone turned to look at Samson, who slowly stood free of the doorframe, came fully inside, and slid into one of the open seats.

Joe opened his Bible and did his best to continue. Emotions swarmed his head and he had to push them down. He had no choice but to read from his notes.

He fumbled in his Bible, flipping the pages to and fro, looking for the hastily written notes while he felt like a million sets of eyes were upon him, as though they were watching and waiting for him to fail.

Why was everything so silent?

Joe's mouth went dry.

Thankfully, he remembered he'd asked for a glass of water and Amy had set it on a table to one side. He took two steps to it and took a quick mouthful.

When he set the glass down, fearful thoughts raced through his head.

Had someone told his uncle that he was doing a bad job and Samson had come to replace him?

Then someone else appeared in the doorway.

It was Mike.

The storekeeper gave him a smile and a wave. He nodded back to him and one of the community members saw Mike and silently greeted him and Mike was invited to sit down. Seeing Mike's friendly face on one side and Amy and Delia smiling at him on the other side of the room, he was able to relax.

Joe said a quick silent prayer and opened his mouth.

Twenty minutes later, the sermon was finished. All had gone well except for the timing. The sermons normally went for forty-five minutes and Joe's was finished in half the time. That was not what he'd planned, but it was how it'd turned out. He closed his Bible, amazed that his uncle, or anyone, could talk for forty-five minutes. After that, he sat down and Mr. King the deacon took over.

As Joe sat and listened to another man sing a hymn in

High German, he couldn't get over the feeling that these people had traveled a long distance and would they think that it wasn't worth it for such a short meeting? Would they come to the next meeting?

He felt a complete failure.

As soon as the deacon closed the meeting in prayer, some of the women got up to organize the food. Then everyone stood up and a couple of men approached him telling him they had enjoyed what he'd said.

He was grateful for their words, but he was sure they were only being polite. He looked around for Mike and saw him talking to people already, so he swallowed hard and walked over to his disagreeable cousin. It was typical that his cousin would be standing by himself at the back of the room. His downcast face wasn't a welcoming sight.

"Samson, what are you doing here?"

"I came to help out Uncle Luke. What else would I be doing here?"

"That's what I'm doing. No need for both of us to be here."

"I wouldn't say that. Two are better than one, don't you think?"

"No, I don't. Does Uncle Luke know you're here?"

"I think you should be calling him Bishop Luke under the circumstances. Shows more respect, don't you think so?"

"Does he know you're here?" Joe repeated, choosing not to say that Samson had just referred to the bishop as 'Uncle Luke.'

"Yes, of course he does. I think he asked me before he asked you. I didn't think I could be here, but then I finally got a gap in my busy schedule, so of course I got here as soon as I could."

"Where are you staying?"

"With you in Bishop Luke's house, of course. I knew before I got here there'd be no other accommodation in this one-horse town."

Joe sighed.

"You don't look too happy, Joe. I'm only here to help, not hinder. Or have you forgotten how to smile these days?"

"Look, what are you really doing here? It's no secret we've never gotten along, so why are you doing this?"

"Now let's not make this about you and me. It's about helping someone out, and I'll do what I can."

Joe couldn't help thinking his cousin was there solely to give him a hard time. "Is there any other reason you're here?"

"Like what? What are you talking about?"

"Good morning, stand-in-bishop," said a familiar voice.

When Joe turned his back on his cousin, he saw Mike, his hands tucked into his pockets. "Well, you were late, but it's a pleasure to see you. I wasn't sure you'd come, but I'm glad you did." Joe extended his hand toward his friend.

Mike shook Joe's hand firmly. "Thank you. I figured I'd check it out. It was different than I had expected."

"Oh, well, I hope that's a good thing."

"It is, I think I could handle it on a regular basis," he said, a hint of laughter in his voice.

"For some people, finding the Lord is a journey of

discovery. You're free to come whenever you'd like, we're not here to force things on you or anyone else."

"We'll see," Mike said.

"Well, you're more than welcome anytime." When Joe saw Mike was focused on something, he turned around and saw Delia and Amy walking toward them.

"I know they're not coming to talk to me," Joe whispered, "and anyway, I should get to know some of these folks."

"Sure. I'll go as soon as I talk with Amy."

"You might as well stay for a bite to eat."

"Thank you. I will, if that's okay."

Mike was then joined by Delia and Amy as the older women brought the food they'd prepared at the house and set it on two large tables at the back.

Before Joe got too far, Samson confronted him.

"Nice of you to introduce me to that man," Samson said, full of his usual sarcasm.

"Oh him? That was Mike from the store across the road. Sorry, everyone from around here knows him. I guess that's why I didn't think to introduce him."

"I enjoyed what you said, Joe."

Joe smiled. "I tried, but it might have been too short."

"Sometimes it's better to get one small thing realized than to stand and preach for as long as possible."

Joe took that to be some kind of encouragement. Maybe his cousin had changed. If that was so, Joe knew he had to find it in his heart to change toward him too. "Tell me, Samson, what are you really doing here? Perhaps if you come clean with me, we can somehow come to an agreement where we get along."

Samson didn't answer, as he was too busy staring at Delia. Or, was it Amy? He finally said, "Is this the real reason you're here, Joe? You're keeping a secret from your family? You're here because of Delia. Your folks would love to know that. I remember you and she had a thing going."

CHAPTER EIGHT

*J*oe stared at Samson. "Delia? No, you've got it all wrong. She's here because she's the new teacher."

Hearing her name, Delia glanced up at them. She left off talking to Amy and Mike and walked over. "I thought it was you, Samson. You're Joe's cousin, right? I met you a few times when you visited him over the years."

"Hello, Delia. Sadly, it's true, I am Joe's cousin."

Joe's eyebrows drew together at his comment, while Delia giggled.

Samson held himself differently in front of Delia. "What brings you here?"

"I'm the schoolteacher here now. I start soon after Christmas."

"Are you married yet, Delia?"

Delia giggled again and this time she fluttered her dark eyelashes. "No, I'm not. How about you?"

"No."

"That's a surprise. I thought you would've been

married by now, Samson. What happened to Becky Yoder? She's a friend of my cousin, and… I was sure she said you two were getting married."

Samson raised his hands. "You shouldn't listen to gossip. I didn't marry her. Let's just say I'm keeping my options open."

"Is that what they call it these days?" Joe said.

"It's a plan. At least I have one." Samson frowned at Joe and then gave Delia a big smile.

"Are you on vacation?" Delia asked Samson.

"Hardly. No, I've come to help out my Uncle Luke. Bishop Luke, I should say."

"That's nice. He's got the two of you helping."

When Delia saw Joe looking down at his feet seeming even more uncomfortable, she thought it best to leave. "I should go and help with the food."

As she walked away, Samson called after her, "I'll find you later and we can talk some more, Delia, if that's okay."

She turned around with a big smile. "Okay."

When Delia was gone, Samson grunted at Joe, "Were you trying to keep her a secret?"

"What do you mean?"

"You came out here knowing she'd be here."

"No, don't be ridiculous. She's not my kind at all."

"Not your kind?"

"I mean not my type."

"I say she is. She'd be anyone's type. I know Delia has a cousin too—not the gossiping one—an attractive one. Is that her?" He nodded to Amy, who was still talking with Mike.

"That's right. Her name's Amy. You've got a good memory since you would've met Amy only once, ages ago."

"I've got a good memory for pretty girls."

Joe couldn't believe his ears. He didn't want Samson involved with either Amy or Delia. He didn't know any woman who deserved a man as fake as Samson. He was wrong about his cousin having changed. He hadn't, not at all. Everything that came out of his mouth was an annoyance.

It amazed him such a devious man as Samson was still in the Amish community, and thought of highly by his relatives including his uncle.

Then some other men came up and Joe introduced them to Samson.

Joe left Samson talking to them while he went to talk to others.

In the midst of helping with the food, Delia was also talking to the crowd of children who'd gathered around her.

Soon, she was crouching down, talking to them at their level.

Joe noticed how her face lit up when she was around them. A lady then told them not to bother Delia so much and the children dispersed.

Delia stood up and caught Joe's eye, and he looked away. She didn't know why he looked so uncomfortable right now. It was plain to see that something was going on between him and Samson. Joe had been visibly shaken when Samson arrived at the meeting. It wasn't merely that he had been shocked to see him, it was much more than that.

When she was talking with them just now, she could tell by the way Joe clenched his jaw. And Samson clearly seemed to know it and to be playing on it.

Her best guess was they had rivalry between them. She'd seen that in her students who were brothers and sometimes cousins. When she noticed Joe walking off, she hurried to catch him before he started talking to someone else. "Joe."

He looked over at her and smiled. "Yes, Delia?"

"I think we should have everybody who's involved in the play meet somewhere tomorrow evening, and we should announce that today while everybody is here."

He nodded slowly. "Good idea. And who would be involved?"

"Well, I'm not sure. I'll have to ask Amy. Perhaps everybody could meet at your place at seven. Is that okay?"

"Yes, seven's fine."

He went to walk away, and she said, "Just one more thing."

Turning back, he asked, "What's that?"

"How about Amy and I cook dinner for you tomorrow at your place? We can have an early dinner before everybody else arrives."

A smile spread across his face. "Good, I like the sound of that. Thank you. Only thing is I now have Samson staying with me."

"Oh, he's staying with you?"

"That's right."

"Okay, that's easy, we'll make it a dinner for four. And maybe we should be at your place at four in the afternoon? Does that suit?"

"Come whatever time you like, anytime that suits you. I don't think I've got anywhere to be tomorrow."

"That's wonderful. Thanks Joe. I'm so excited about the play. I've already started writing it."

"There's not much time for everyone to learn their lines."

"I'm making it easy. Don't worry. They also don't have to say their lines exactly. It'll all work. I have full confidence so don't worry."

"Okay. I'll try not to."

She laughed. "When you are worried, you have two lines between your eyes, reaching upward."

His mouth dropped open and she hurried away.

Now, he couldn't even frown without getting self-conscious. However, he was pleased she was treating him as though he was in charge and not Samson. He knew in his heart that Samson was there to try his best to take over.

CHAPTER NINE

*D*elia noticed Amy and Mike were deep in conversation. Then Mike suddenly walked out the door. Delia walked over to her, and then whispered, "Amy, what about Joe's cousin, Samson? He said he's come to help out. Joe doesn't seem too happy that he's here."

"Why? What did he say?"

"Nothing, but I could tell from the way his body stiffened."

Amy shrugged. "Bishop Luke didn't mention anything to Dad about someone else coming."

"It seems like a new development then. What are your thoughts of him? He's handsome, *jah*? I can see the two of you together."

Amy laughed. "I don't think so."

"He is so. Don't you like anyone? Don't you want to get married?"

"Of course I do."

"Well you have to take your opportunities where you

can, you know. Unless you plan on traveling around and getting to meet more people... do you?"

"No. I haven't got any plans to go anywhere."

"That means *Gott* will have to bring you a man. Bring him to your door. Maybe Samson's the one for you."

Amy shrugged her shoulders. "If you say so."

"I thought you'd show more enthusiasm for that. I thought of you as soon as I saw him."

"What about you?" Amy asked.

She couldn't bear to tell her cousin that she still liked Joe in case Amy liked him too. "No I don't think he's for me."

"Why are you trying to palm him off on me, then?"

"I'm just helping, that's all. Anyway, we'll get to know him better because tomorrow night I'm cooking the dinner at the bishop's house and then we're going to talk about the play. Oh, that reminds me. We've got to get a few people to join us for tomorrow night. Who do you think would want to be in the play? Are there some people who act in the play every year?"

"There are."

"School children?"

"No, we've already had the children's play for the year last month. This one is just for the adults."

"That is disappointing. But I guess adults would be easier to direct than children."

"You'll soon find out."

"Hey, I'm only helping, I'm not running the show."

Joe walked up to them. "Am I interrupting something?"

"No. Amy's about to find people to take part in the

play and ask them to be here tomorrow night."

"Thank you, Amy. It all hinges on you two ladies. I know nothing about this kind of thing."

"Delia has the hard part of writing the play. It would be easier if we did the same one as last year," Amy said.

Delia's face soured. "There's no way we can do that. I can't believe you think that would be okay."

"You're going to have a very busy day tomorrow," Joe said to Delia.

"I'll wake up early and work on it all day."

"I'll see you tomorrow." Joe moved away from them.

Once he was gone, Delia said to her cousin, "I told him I'd cook dinner for him tomorrow night. Him and his cousin. We're to be there at four. I guess I was assuming you'd help me. Is that okay with you?"

"*Jah*, that's ok. Sounds like fun, in fact."

"Good, *denke*. And then we'll stay on for the first play run-through. Don't you think it will be nice having dinner, just the four of us, two single males and two single females?"

"I guess so."

"Take another look at Samson."

Amy stared at him. "I suppose he is... handsome."

"Of course he is, and I'm sure you'll like his personality too. Now hurry and invite the people who're going to act in the play. Tell them to be here at seven and not before. We don't want anyone ruining our double date."

Amy narrowed her eyes. "Don't call it that."

"All right, all right. Just go. Tell them it's going to be our first rehearsal night, kind of."

Amy did as Delia said.

CHAPTER TEN

 fter breakfast the next morning, Delia sat down at a small desk in the living room corner where her aunt spent many an hour writing letters. As she sat with pen poised above the page, she knew she didn't want the play to be like every other play they'd had. Then she decided. The play would be about the Samaritan she'd mentioned to Joe. He'd liked the story as well.

The good thing about working with that story was, if anyone forgot their lines, it would be easy to make them up on the spot and nobody would know any different.

After two hours, Delia had outlined the play and she could visualize how she wanted it acted out.

Aunt Sylvia brought her a cup of tea. "How's it coming along?"

"Fine, thank you. Oh, do you need your desk back?"

"No, you sit there as long as you need. There's nothing more important than the yearly play. It's the highlight of the year"

"Oh my, that makes me nervous." Delia looked down at the pale pink teacup.

"Don't be." Aunt Sylvia sat down on the couch with a cup of tea of her own. "I know you'll do a good job. You're so brave coming here to our small town. We appreciate you being here."

"I did get a good welcome. Everyone's so friendly."

"We are so glad to have you here. I just want you to know that."

"Thank you," Delia said before she took a sip of her tea. "I think this is where God wants me to be."

"I don't doubt it for a minute." Sylvia set her teacup and saucer on the small table in front of her and then picked up a needlework sampler.

Delia heard noises in the kitchen and guessed Amy was baking something.

"Just let me know if you want me to do some chores or help with something."

"No, you do what you're doing. It's important work."

"Thank you. I'll have a break for a moment while I drink the tea." Delia stood up and stretched, and then sat back down.

"Did you see the new man yesterday? I heard he's Joe's cousin. Another one of Bishop Luke's nephews."

"That's right, he is. His name is Samson Bontrager."

Amy came into the room wiping her hands on her apron. "Who are you talking about?"

"We're talking about Samson, Joe's cousin."

"I'm just figuring out why he's here," Aunt Sylvia said.

"I think he's here to help out, isn't he, Delia."

"That's right. That's what he said, but it seems Joe didn't know he was coming."

Sylvia stared at her daughter and then her niece. "Or perhaps God directed him here for a certain reason. It's not often we get visitors who are so handsome and just the right age for you. Then there's also Joe."

"Oh, don't you start with that again, *Mamm*." Amy placed her hands on her hips, then turned and said to Delia, "My parents are always trying to marry me off."

"Mine are no different. They haven't had any success yet, though." Delia laughed.

"Neither have mine."

"The trouble with you girls today is that you're too fussy."

Amy sat down with her mother. "I don't think we're fussy, it's just that we've not met the right ones yet."

Sylvia rolled her eyes. "I hope you don't leave it too long."

"It will be in God's timing," Amy said.

"Well, I just haven't had any to choose from and then... I just hope I haven't made a mistake coming here." Delia took a sip of tea.

"Whatever do you mean, Delia?"

Delia sighed, placing the cup back onto the saucer. "I don't know. I just doubt myself so much sometimes. I thought God wanted me here because there was a certain man here to match me with as well as me coming here to teach."

"It's quite possible that's why you're here. For both of those reasons. You'll have to wait and see. Now there are two unmarried men who have come when you've showed up. One just before and one just after."

Amy remained silent. So, Delia wondered, did her cousin like Joe… or not? She was so hard to read when she was quiet like that.

"How's the play going?" Aunt Sylvia asked again.

"Pretty good. Do you both want to help me? I'll tell you what I've got so far. I have to have it finished by tonight, or most of it done anyway, so we can talk about it at Joe's place when all the people come. I should call them actors because that's what they are."

"We'd love to help, wouldn't we, Amy?"

"Of course."

Delia picked up her pages, took a deep breath, stood up and read her play. In between some of the lines, she acted out how she would direct the actors. In some places, she overacted the parts, causing Amy and her mother to laugh at her.

When Delia was finished, she sat down, facing them expectantly waiting to hear what they thought.

"I *like* it," Amy said.

"Me too. Very entertaining."

Delia was happy, and happier still that they hadn't suggested any changes. "It will be better once it's acted out by different people in the costumes and all. I still have a few adjustments to make, but I think I'm pleased with most of it."

Amy said, "Don't forget that Mike said he'd stop by sometime this morning to tell you how much the apartment is going to be."

"Yes, that's right. I remembered it early this morning,

but then I forgot it when I started in on the play, until you mentioned it just now."

"Don't worry," said her aunt, "you'll still have all day to work on the play. When Mike visits he never stays for long. Now, Delia, what about the costumes?"

Amy said, "We will have enough costumes from before, so we should be fine."

"I suppose so, but since it's Christmas it just seems to make sense to do the baby in the manger, the star in the sky and the wise men coming to visit the young baby, Jesus. It's the whole Christmas message."

Delia was downcast. Her aunt didn't like her play and thought they should do the same old play year after year. "I know, but I just wanted to do something different."

"I'm sure it will be good," Uncle Thomas said, as he walked into the house from feeding the horses. "And you're right, it doesn't hurt to have something different sometimes. You're bringing a good refreshing change to this community, Delia."

Delia smiled. "I hope so. I really do. I like what I've seen of it already."

"It is a very pretty town," said Amy.

"And you'll see that when Joe shows you around," Thomas said with a grin.

"I just hope he doesn't think I'm wasting his time."

"Nonsense. He'd be delighted to do it. I saw the look on his face and he was pleased."

"I agree with that," Aunt Sylvia said.

"When is he showing you around Delia?"

"I'm not quite sure. Perhaps we'll find out tonight over dinner."

"I admire the way you've come here and pulled up your sleeves and started doing work for the community. You wasted no time taking charge of the play."

Delia was delighted with his words of appreciation. It made her feel she had made the right choice coming to Stinterton. "I'm only pleased I'm able to help while the bishop's not here. Everyone gave me such a lovely welcome, and the children I'll be teaching are delightful. I'm going to love getting to know them better."

When they heard a car, Amy jumped up and headed to the door. "That's him now."

"Who?" Thomas asked.

"Mike, I'd say," Sylvia answered.

Amy opened the door. "Yes, it's Mike."

"Have him sit here in the living room so we all can hear what he has to say," Thomas said.

Delia moved away from the desk and sat on the couch. She found it a little odd that they'd want to know how much rent she was paying. In her mind, it should've been her business alone. Even her parents wouldn't have interfered with that. It seemed her aunt and uncle thought differently.

"I'll bring him in," Amy said as she disappeared out the door.

While they waited, Delia asked, "Is there anything I should ask him? I haven't done this kind of thing before. I've only lived at my parents' house."

Aunt Sylvia said, "We'll have to know if there are any other charges, such as the use of gas, or whether that's included in the price he tells you."

Uncle Thomas added, "And you mentioned you need a

horse and buggy. When you get one, where will you keep it?"

"He said there are plenty of places I can keep a horse and a buggy."

"But will that be included in the lease amount as well, or will that be extra?"

"Oh yes, that's right. It would be easier if he gave me a price that included everything."

"Then that's what we shall ask him."

Aunt Sylvia took another sip of tea. "What is keeping Amy? Also, Delia, will you have your own separate entrance? You don't want to be walking through Mike's parents' house every time you go up to your little apartment."

"No, that would be dreadful. There is an entrance from the shop and I'm sure he said there was one from outside as well."

"We'll have to check on that," her uncle said.

A couple of minutes later, Amy brought Mike into the room. When they had exchanged greetings with Mike, he sat down in an armchair and Amy sat down next to Delia.

"Thanks for stopping by, Mike. Have you worked out a price yet?" Sylvia asked.

Thomas leaned forward. "Before you say anything, Delia wants a price that includes everything. She wants to keep a horse and buggy there so she will need a suitable stable and yard. Also a place to store the horse's feed and straw, and she'd want the price to include that, too."

"And gas," Sylvia added. "We're hoping there is a separate entrance to the apartment, too, so that she doesn't have to go through your place to get to hers."

Delia just sat there waiting while her aunt and uncle went back and forth with questions and requests.

Finally, they stopped and Mike had a chance to talk. "Ah, all very good points. I told Delia we'd work out a place for her horse and buggy, that's not a problem. We've got many pastures and sheds, stables and barns that we've used over the years on our forty acres. We don't use most of them anymore, but we keep them in good condition. And the price would include the gas, and yes there is an entrance around the back with stairs that lead up to her room. She doesn't have to go anywhere near my place to get to hers."

Sylvia's eyebrows rose. "Room? I thought you said it was more than just a room, Delia?"

She looked at her aunt's worried face. "That's right. It is more than a room."

Mike chuckled. "I don't know why I call it a room. I've always just called it a room, but it's much more than that."

"So the price?" Delia asked.

Mike then mentioned a figure which was much lower than Delia had expected, but maybe it was normal for the small town.

"That sounds reasonable. Don't you think so, Uncle Thomas?"

"I agree."

"Great," Mike said, "you can move in any time you like, Delia."

Uncle Thomas leaned forward. "Just a moment. There's a matter of the electrical wiring. That would all have to be taken out. Would that be a problem?" He raised one eyebrow as he stared at Mike.

Mike scratched the back of his neck. "I know the place was separately wired when we had people living up there some time ago, so I don't think it would be a problem. The only issue would be finding someone to do all that. The man we could've used is away until February."

"And who would pay for that?"

"We'll cover it. Delia won't have to pay."

Uncle Thomas leaned back, smiling. "It's settled then. You get that done, and Delia can stay here until February."

Delia couldn't wait that long to be out on her own. "There must be someone else who could do electrical work in this town, wouldn't there be?"

"One of the men in the community can do it," Aunt Sylvia said. "It can't be that hard."

"My folks won't let anyone do anything unless they're properly licensed for it, and I wouldn't think any of your community members would be certified to work on electricity since they're not allowed to have it in their houses and such."

"He's right, Sylvia."

"I was just thinking of it as being part of the building process."

"Leave it with me," Mike said. "I'm sure I'll be able to find somebody to do it if you're in a hurry, Delia."

She didn't want to offend her aunt and uncle. "I'm not exactly in a hurry. It's just that I imagined I'd be living by myself when I moved out of my parents' place."

"I can understand that," said Amy. "Of course you'd want to be a grown-up and by yourself and all that."

"I know what you mean, and I understand," Uncle Thomas said.

"Should I make a payment now, Mike?"

Her uncle shook his head. "Wait until the job is done."

Mike smiled at her. "That's right. No hurry. Maybe you can stop by soon and have a look at the horse and buggy accommodation options. Together we can work out where you can keep them and the horse's feed, and things like that."

"That's a good idea," Amy said. "We could go there this afternoon, Delia. Before we go to Joe's for dinner and the play rehearsal."

"Okay. It's not really a rehearsal yet, I suppose, but, *jah,* we can do that. As long as Mike's got the time."

"Anytime this afternoon will be fine. I'll be on my way then so I can find someone who can do this electrical work."

Thomas stood up. "Thank you, Mike, and say hello to your folks for me."

"Stay for a cup of coffee, Mike?" Sylvia asked.

"Thank you, but I should go."

Amy jumped to her feet. "I'll walk you out."

CHAPTER ELEVEN

"*D*elia, we have plenty of chickens you can take to Joe's place to cook for the evening meal."

Delia hoped she wouldn't hurt her aunt's feelings. It seemed they ate a lot of chicken. "Thank you, but I want to buy something and pay for it myself."

"Is this part of you wanting to feel grown up?"

Delia had to smile. Didn't her aunt realize she was already grown up? "Probably."

"Well, what will you cook?"

"I'll just go to the store and see what they have. I'll do that on the way there. Is that okay with you, Amy?"

"Sure, as long as you don't mind not knowing what you're cooking until the last minute."

"That's okay, I'll play it by ear."

"If that's what you want," Aunt Sylvia said, "but you'll probably still end up with chicken. You can cook a wonderful variety of meals with chicken."

"I know, that's true, but I'd still like to see what they have."

"I can't stop you. I will insist you take some vegetables with you. We have so many."

"Thank you, Aunt Sylvia. I will do that."

Uncle Thomas said, "We can give you money, Delia. No need to spend your savings since you're not working yet. How many people will you be feeding?"

"Only the four of us. The other people will be coming after the meal."

"Ah, good idea."

"And thank you, Uncle Thomas, but I have enough money. I worked right up until a few weeks ago."

He grunted. "You're a stubborn girl, you always were."

Delia laughed. "I don't know about that."

"Amy will help you pack a box of vegetables."

"Thank you, Aunt Sylvia."

In the early afternoon, Amy and Delia hitched the buggy and headed off with a box of vegetables, as well as two cherry pies that Sylvia insisted they take for dessert.

As they headed down the road, Amy said, "Do you think two pies will be enough?"

Delia laughed. "That'll be plenty. There will only be four of us. Oh wait. I suppose we should get something to feed everyone who's coming to the rehearsal. Just some cookies will be enough, as everyone will have had dinner. I'll have to see what they've got at the store."

"They have most things there. What are you thinking of having for the main meal tonight?"

Delia shrugged. "That's the trouble. I probably won't know until I see it."

They soon arrived at the store. When they walked in,

Mike looked happy to see them. He came out from behind the counter and walked over to them.

"Hello again, Delia and Amy."

"Hi, Mike. I'm looking for something to feed four people tonight. I'm cooking over at Joe's place."

"And I'm helping," Amy said.

He gave Amy a big smile before he turned his attention back to Delia. "What are you thinking of?"

"I'm not sure. I have a stack of vegetables that my aunt made me bring, so we're all right for those. Maybe some kind of meat, and then I'll have to decide how to cook it."

"Chicken?" he asked.

Delia shook her head with a laugh.

"I have some nice lamb that just came in."

"Lamb?"

"Yes, you can do all sorts of things with that, braise it, stew it, bake it."

"Bake! Is that the same thing as roast?"

Amy said, "It is the same."

"Roast lamb and roasted vegetables. That's what we'll have tonight." She turned to Amy. "What do you think?"

"I think that would be wonderful."

"Good, that's what we'll have."

"I've got a nice leg of lamb. I'll just get it from out back."

When he left, Delia said, "I think I'm going to enjoy living around here."

"And how convenient will it be to live above the store?"

"I know. If I run out of anything, I won't have far to go.

But, do you think it will be practical, as a long-term thing for me? Could I live above a store forever?"

"I don't see why not, and you need to be realistic about it, you'll only be here until you meet the right man. That is, if the man isn't from around here. He might sweep you away and take you to where he's from."

Delia smiled at the thought, knowing the right man could be closer than he'd ever been. "That's true… do you think I will meet someone?" She was fishing again to see if her cousin would admit to liking Joe. Amy was so hard to read.

"Of course you will. It's only a matter of time." Amy stood on her tiptoes looking out the doorway Mike had gone through. "Where's Mike gone?"

"To get the meat, he said."

"I'll just see if he needs any help." Amy started walking off.

"Hey Amy, you can't go back there, can you?"

"I won't be long. You look after the store if anyone comes in."

"Me?"

And just like that, Amy was gone. Delia couldn't believe how impatient Amy was when they hadn't even given Joe a time for their arrival. What was her hurry?

Delia filled in her time looking at cookies and candies that might be suitable for a late-night snack after supper. After a couple of minutes, Amy rushed back through the doorway.

"There's been a disaster here, Delia!"

"What is it?"

"Mike's freezer has broken down and everything has

thawed out leaving a dreadful mess everywhere. He said for you to take this and there'll be no charge." She handed Delia a white plastic bag.

Delia put the cookies back down to free her hands, and then she looked inside the bag to see a decent sized leg of lamb. "I can't just take it. I have the money to pay."

"Do it. He said it'll only go to waste."

Delia looked down at the meat and put her hand around the outside of the bag to feel the leg. "But this isn't frozen."

Amy looked down. "It's not. That's right, but that came from the refrigerated area. It's the frozen area that's broken."

What Amy said made no sense. Maybe if she hadn't bought it, it would've gone into the freezer. "Is Mike coming out?"

"No. I offered to stay and help him with the mess. I'll be over later when I'm done. Drive the buggy across to Joe's, would you?"

Delia whispered, "Can't his parents help him?"

"They're too old. I don't mind doing it."

"All right." Delia looked on the bright side. Now she had a chance to impress Joe with her cooking skills. "Okay. Are you sure Mike doesn't need another pair of hands?"

"No, Dee. You've too much to do. I will only be an hour or so and then I'll be over to help."

"Okay." Delia raised up the bag of meat. "Please thank Mike for this, would you? But I need something for after supper too."

Amy frowned and then raced to the aisle where the

cookies were. She grabbed three packages of cookies and placed them on top of the meat Delia was holding. "I'll pay Mike for these before I come over. Now go. I'll be over as soon as I can."

Delia walked out the door and got into the buggy. She'd never seen someone so eager to get rid of her. There must've been a huge mess to clean.

CHAPTER TWELVE

*J*oe was giving the kitchen an extra cleaning when he saw Thomas's horse and buggy leave the store and continue to the house. He looked again and saw it was Delia by herself. He left what he was doing and went outside to meet her.

When the horse stopped, he took hold of the reins and looped them over the hitching post.

She jumped down from the buggy. "Joe, something terrible has happened."

He stared at her hoping someone wasn't hurt. "What is it?"

"The freezer in Mike's store has broken down. It must've been a huge mess everywhere."

"Oh, you had me worried for a minute." He wanted to give her the hint not to overreact like that in the future. "You mean no one's ill or injured?"

"No, that would be dreadful. I would've told you that first up."

She clearly wasn't the kind of person who took a hint.

"By the way you were talking I thought something dreadful had happened."

"It is that way for Mike and his folks. They could've lost hundreds of dollars' worth of food. A whole freezer full of food, gone to waste."

"Let's get inside, it's chilly out here. Was there much food in the freezer?"

"I don't know, there must've been because Amy is staying there to help him clean up the mess."

"Ah. That explains it. I wondered why Amy wasn't with you. Er, did you see this broken freezer for yourself?"

"Of course not. It was in the back room, not in the store."

"Hmm."

She headed to the back of the buggy. "Would you mind getting the box of vegetables out of the back?" She lifted up the white bag she'd placed next to the box and then grabbed the cookies and placed them in her fabric bag that already contained notebooks and pens. "Mark was kind enough to give me a leg of lamb, no charge."

"That was good of him, but don't you mean Mike?"

"Oh no. I hope I haven't been calling him Mark all the time."

Joe chuckled as he lifted out the vegetables. "I'm sure he won't mind if you did." He closed the buggy door by leaning his body against it.

"Everybody is so nice around here. I'm going to love living here."

He carried the goods through the house and into the kitchen where he placed them down on the countertop.

"Are you going to need some help with the cooking now that Amy's not here?"

She laughed loudly. "No. I can cook on my own."

"Okay, well I'll leave you to it and I'll get on with something else."

"Yes. Why don't you do that?"

The cat walked into the kitchen meowing.

"Oh, she's hungry, Joe."

"I've fed her twice already today."

Delia frowned and looked down at her. "I'd say she's going to have those kittens any day now."

Joe narrowed his eyes. "I'd say she'll have ten, she's so big."

"Does she use that cave I made her?"

"I wouldn't know. She's been coming in the house a lot lately. I don't know if she's allowed to do that. I got no instructions about anything. I'm just making it up as I go along."

"Well, I think you'll have to feed her for a third time."

"Okay." He grabbed some meat from the gas-powered fridge and finely chopped it. Then he put it in her bowl in the corner of the kitchen.

"If you don't want her to come inside, you shouldn't feed her inside."

"I'm only feeding her here because she's inside. That happened first, not the other way around." He left the room before she could say anything more.

Delia turned on the gas oven to heat it. Then she looked in the box her aunt had given her to find some herbs. She mixed herbs with butter and covered the lamb.

Then she found a large baking tray and placed the lamb inside. It was a perfect fit.

Once she popped it in the oven, she washed her hands and set about cutting the vegetables, humming as she went and thankful her aunt had already washed them.

Joe sat down looking at some bills that his uncle had gotten a few days before. He'd have to call these people and explain that his uncle was ill. Hopefully, they'd understand and delay their payment requests. Then, Joe was unsure of whether his uncle would have wanted him to open his private mail, but it was too late to ask.

His cousin suddenly walked through the front door and sat down opposite.

Joe looked up. "Where have you been?"

Samson shrugged his shoulders. "Out walking."

"In this cold?"

"It's not cold. This is nothing." He must've heard Delia's humming because he looked toward the kitchen. "We have a visitor?"

"We do."

"I saw the buggy out front. I thought you might be going somewhere."

"No. It's Delia. She's cooking dinner for us and after that, we have people coming to talk about the play."

"What play?"

"The Christmas play. Seems they have one every year. They tell me everyone comes from miles around to see it."

Samson rolled his eyes. "What a complete waste of time." He leaned back on the couch and stretched his legs out, crossing them over on the coffee table.

Joe couldn't help noticing his dirty boots. Then Samson sat up straight. "Delia you said?"

"Yes."

Samson smiled. "She's by herself?"

"She's the only one in the kitchen until Amy gets here."

"I could get used to this. I love the sound of her. I'd love nothing more than a woman like her to cook for me every night. She sounds so happy and she's not a bad looker, wouldn't you say?"

Joe couldn't help frowning. Since when did his cousin care about what he thought? "I guess so."

Without saying another word, Samson sprang to his feet with his gaze fixed on the kitchen.

Joe sat there, frozen. Had he missed something about Delia? He hoped she wouldn't fall for his cousin. He wasn't keen on Delia, but something inside him didn't want her to like Samson. In a split-second Joe recalled how Samson had led two women to believe he'd marry them and with each one, he called off the wedding just two weeks before. Would Delia end up being jilted woman number three?

He'd have to warn her about him. "Hey, Samson."

Samson turned around. "What?"

"Keep away from her."

Samson walked closer to him. "Why would you say that?"

"She's not your type."

"How would you know what my type is? You don't want her. You said she's not *your* type."

When Joe didn't answer, Samson grunted, "You're

ridiculous. I'm going to my room. I'll talk to her when you're not around to interrupt."

After twenty minutes or so, Delia walked out of the kitchen. "There you are."

Joe looked up. "I'm still here."

"What are you thinking about? You look like you're deep in thought."

"I'm just reeling after giving that dreadful sermon yesterday."

She sat down on the couch next to him, admiring his humility. Not many men would open up and reveal their true thoughts. "Don't say that. It wasn't dreadful."

"I feel it was."

"I didn't think so. I enjoyed it."

He smiled. "I'm pleased to hear it."

"Do you mind if I do some work on the play while I'm here?"

"Of course you can, you don't have to ask me. That's why you're here."

"Good. Because the meat will take quite a while to cook. A couple of hours at least. And it'll take me that long to get all my thoughts in order before people arrive here tonight."

"I know how that feels." He offered a crooked smile.

She reached down into her bag on the floor beside the couch and pulled out her notebook and started reading.

"While you're doing that, I'll see how Mike and Amy are getting along with the broken freezer."

"Okay."

Worried about Mike having a big crush on Amy and spending too much time with her, Joe left his uncle's place and sprinted across the road to see what was really going on.

He pushed open the door of the shop and saw Mike's father's smiling face. He'd met Mike and his parents on the first day he arrived. "Ah, he's got you working today has he, Jimmy?"

"Yes. Mike and Amy are doing what they can to fix the broken freezer."

"Fixing it?"

"Cleaning up the mess, I should say. We won't know if it's able to be fixed until the mechanic gets here next week. We called, but at this time of year…"

"I get it." Then Joe realized the broken freezer story was actually true. "I hope you didn't lose too much food."

Jimmy shook his head. "It's not looking good."

"I'm sorry to hear that. I've come to offer a hand."

"Thank you. Go on through that door to the back. I'll take you."

Jimmy led Joe through the doorway into the residence. They walked past Mike's mother who was watching TV.

"Good afternoon," Joe said.

"Oh hello, Joe isn't it?"

"That's right." He continued following Mike's father through the house into the back room where there was a large storage room with a walk-in freezer.

He found Amy mopping, and Mike had long plastic gloves and rubber boots on as he was throwing objects into large trash cans.

Joe stood there not knowing what to say. Mike and Amy looked over at him.

"Joe, you've come to help?" Mike asked.

Jimmy turned around and said as he left, "I'll go back to the store."

"Thanks, Dad."

"I came to help, but it looks like I'm too late."

"No you're not. There is another mop over there." Amy pointed to the second mop.

"Don't you have visitors tonight?" asked Mike.

"I do, but Delia has everything under control."

Joe got busy and helped them mop up all the excess moisture.

An hour later, shelves were wiped down, food was fitted into two large fridges, and the floor was nearly dry.

"Thank you to the both of you. Now that we've done that, I'll get my mother to make us a cup of something hot. Ma," he yelled out.

"Yeah?"

"Make us three coffees, would you please? And find some cake?"

"Give me five minutes. My show's nearly finished."

Mike smiled. "Sorry about that. My mother loves those daytime TV shows. There's a bathroom just in there if you want to wash your hands or anything."

"You go first, Amy," Joe said.

When they'd all cleaned up, they sat around the kitchen table.

The kettle whistled and Mike's mother walked in. "Everything fixed?" she asked.

"It is."

As she made the coffee, she said, "I want to thank you both for helping. Mike's got a lot to do around here now that his father and I are older. And we're not getting any younger. The place will be his one day and it'll be a hard job for him to run on his own."

"I'll manage, Ma."

"I know you will, because you're always saying you will, so I've come to believe it. Coffee for everyone?"

"Yes please," Amy said.

"And for me," Joe agreed.

CHAPTER THIRTEEN

"*H*ello."

Delia jumped. She looked up from altering a couple of things in her notes to see Samson. "Hello."

"Did I scare you?" He slid into the chair where Joe had been sitting.

"A little. I thought I was alone in the house. I forgot you were staying here."

"Ah, you forgot me? That must be my problem, all the pretty girls forget me."

She put her hand over her mouth and giggled. "I'm sorry, it's just that I've been so busy writing this Christmas play that I've just blocked everything else out." She looked back at him and saw him as though for the first time. His hazel eyes perfectly complimented his light brown hair.

Then her attention was taken by the bishop's very pregnant cat who'd made herself comfortable in front of the fire. She hadn't noticed her there before because her mind had been fully occupied with something else.

"Tell me what you're doing, what story is the Christmas play? What spin are you putting on it?"

"Well, I think everybody is a little bit shocked that I'm not doing the usual Christmas story. Now I'm second-guessing myself. It's what everybody expects. What if everybody is horribly disappointed?"

"I think what you're doing is wonderful."

"You do?"

"I do."

She smiled. She wanted a man who always agreed with her. That was number one on her list. Things were looking pretty good right now from where she sat. "I could always take a vote with everybody who's coming here tonight."

"Who's coming here tonight?"

"People who will be in the play. They're coming after dinner."

"You were here earlier cooking."

"That's right. We're having a roast tonight. You don't have anywhere else to be, do you?"

"Not when there's a roast on the menu."

She smiled. She was going to enjoy seeing more of him.

"I remember you and your cousin from when I used to visit Joe years back."

She gasped. "I remember you too."

"I've got a pretty good memory for faces."

"What brings you to Stinterton, Samson?"

"I'm helping my cousin out. I was surprised my uncle

didn't ask me, but I came to help out anyway."

"That's good of you. Are you and Joe close?"

She knew by seeing Joe's reaction yesterday that they didn't get along. It didn't make sense he'd come to help Joe. Perhaps it was a case of God intervening on her behalf if he was the man for her.

"As close as cousins can be who only see each other once a year or so."

She opened her book to the back and looked down at her list. Number 2 on the list was that her future husband should be kind. She closed the book and looked up at him. "It was very kind of you to help Joe by coming all the way here. Do you consider yourself a kind person?"

He smiled and his eyes crinkled at the corners. "I couldn't say that about myself or that would be prideful, but others have said that about me. That's all I can say."

That was good enough for her.

"Do you want some help with the play? Why don't you tell me what you've got so far? Use me as your sounding board."

"All right. I'll read you what I have so far." She cleared her throat, opened her book at the first page and started reading. When she finished, she closed her book. "What do you think?"

"I like it."

"Of course, I'll direct people how to play it out. And they will have to be dramatic, really put their heart into it and act well. And, they'll have to remember their lines. I guess they don't have to be word for word as long as they know what's coming next."

"I know what you mean. And you'll be good at telling them how to do that."

She didn't want a false compliment. "Why do you think that?"

"Because you're a schoolteacher. You are used to telling people what to do. And you're good at your job."

"Hmm. And I suppose you heard that from somebody?"

"I know my Uncle Luke, and he wouldn't have you here unless you had come highly recommended."

"I don't know if I did. I guess someone said some nice things about me."

"I know I'm right. That's what I meant." A strange, puzzled look came across his face. He tipped his head upward and wrinkled his nose.

"What's wrong?" she asked.

He sniffed. "What's that smell?"

Delia noticed the room was hazy. It was smoke. "Oh no, it's the dinner!" She raced into the kitchen to see flames inside the oven and smoke billowing out.

She stood there not knowing what to do. Samson moved forward, picked her up and put her to one side. "I'll fix it. Stand back." He covered his hands in hand towels and pulled the pan of flaming meat from the oven, tipped it into the sink, and then turned the tap on.

Delia was still there, staring as the last flames died down and the contents of the sink fizzled loudly.

"Are you okay?" she asked him.

He turned off the gas. "I'm fine. Can't say as much about the dinner."

Delia stepped forward to look at the charred remains.

"That was our dinner. And, I was so busy with the play I forgot about roasting the vegetables. Now we have nothing for dinner."

He looked over his shoulder at the charred remains. "We have burnt offerings."

Delia had to turn around so he wouldn't see her crying. All she wanted to do was make a good impression on everyone. Now all she felt was pressure from the play and pressure for the meal tonight. Why couldn't Amy have been here to help her? She shouldn't have left her to do everything.

"Don't be worried. It's only food."

"I had my mind on the play." She saw the vegetables she was meant to roast lying on the table next to the chopping board. "And the vegetables, I forgot to put them in the oven."

Then they heard the front door open and close. Delia heard talking and knew it was Amy back at last with Joe.

They walked into the kitchen. Joe looked around. "Whoa! I smell smoke."

Amy passed him and rushed to the sink. "What happened, Delia?"

"Well, you weren't here to help and I was busy with the play."

"But how did it burn like this?"

"I don't know."

Joe looked closer at the oven, and touched the dials. "I think it's broken. It's possible it only has a high setting."

Delia knew Joe was finding an excuse for her. "I don't think that's possible. I turned it up too high. I made a mistake. I turned it up high to heat the oven and then I forgot to turn it down when I put the meat in. I'm so sorry everyone. I've ruined dinner, totally."

"Well, Joe, what is there to eat?" Samson asked.

Delia couldn't hold back the tears. She had been trying, but lost the battle and ran out of the room. All she had wanted to do was impress the man who'd turned her down. Maybe make him regret not continuing their relationship.

Amy ran after her and put her arm around her and guided her to the couch.

"It's fine. No one has died. We might miss one meal, so what? I'm sure we can find something else here. I saw vegetables. We can eat those if we put them in a pot to steam right away."

Joe walked into the room. "Don't be upset, Delia. I have ham. I'll make us some ham sandwiches and toast them."

She nodded, not wanting to look at him. "I'm so sorry, Joe."

"No harm done."

"Yes there is," Samson said as he walked into the room. "The flames licked the wall. We'll have to repaint before Uncle Luke comes home."

"Then that's what we'll do," said Joe, "but not tonight. Now if everybody will stay out of the kitchen, I'll make us some toasted sandwiches."

"I'll open some windows to get some of this smoke out," said Samson.

"And I'll steam some vegetables, if that's okay, Joe?" asked Amy. "I saw some of my herbs were still left, too, so I'll add them."

"Sounds good," replied Joe. "If you want to do that, and I'll do my bit."

Delia was horrified that a man was going to cook them dinner. But she was too embarrassed to say or do anything further.

CHAPTER FOURTEEN

*D*elia, Amy, Joe and Samson sat in Bishop Luke's living room munching through their toasted ham sandwiches with the herbed, steamed veggies on the side, while the cat watched them hoping for a handout. The kitchen still smelled too much of smoke to sit in there.

"These are good, Joe," Amy said.

"Thank you. I make them quite often. It's something easy I can make for myself."

"It's good that you have those skills," said Samson.

Joe didn't know if his cousin was being sarcastic or not. He probably was. "Keeps me alive."

"Now tell me, Delia, who is going to be in your play?" Samson asked.

"That's what we're going to decide tonight—who has what part. Would you like to be in it?"

He put his sandwich down and raised up his hands. "No, definitely not. I'd rather be on the sidelines."

Joe grunted. "Yes, he'd rather judge on the sidelines

and tell others what to do rather than actually doing anything himself. It's the way he works."

Amy and Delia exchanged looks. It was clear there was animosity between the men, at least on Joe's side.

Delia tried to change the subject. "It's funny, because here we are two sets of cousins."

"That's right." Amy laughed. "I didn't even realize that. We didn't see enough of each other when we were growing up, did we, Dee?"

"No, but we used to write to each other."

"Are you the same age?" Samson asked.

"I'm a little older than Amy."

"I thought you two were about the same age, like Samson and I are."

"No, I'm three years older. It seemed a big difference when we were younger but it's not so much of a difference now." She looked at Joe. "I feel so bad about burning the meat and filling this place with smoke. I'll come back tomorrow and help fix it."

"Did you say the kitchen needs repainting?" asked Amy. "Dee and I will help."

"It's fine. I can do it by myself while you're both busy with the play and Joe is playing at being a bishop."

Delia looked down at what was left of her sandwich. She didn't know what to say, which was unusual for her, so she picked the ham off the crust and fed it to the cat before she popped the rest into her mouth.

WHEN EVERYONE ARRIVED at the meeting house, Delia told them of her concept for the play. They all seemed delighted to have something different and that gave Delia a whole lot more confidence.

Then they did their first run-through.

It worked out well because Delia managed to find a character for everyone who wanted to be involved, even though some of them didn't have speaking parts. She even got Samson to volunteer for one of those parts, being one person in a crowd.

When the rehearsal was finished, everyone was enjoying the cookies and talking about the play.

"You did a great job, Delia," Samson told her in a loud voice.

Everyone murmured their agreement.

"Thank you. I just did my best, that's all. I hope it turns out good on the night."

"It will," Joe said, smiling.

"How are you settling in, Delia?" Betty Marshal, an older lady, asked her.

"Fine. I have found a place to live, a permanent place. It's above the store across the road here. Now I have everything I need except for a horse and buggy."

"Why would you need one of those?" Joe asked.

Amy said, "That's right, you just walk across the road when you're going to school."

"That's true, I won't need it during the school day, but I don't like to be stuck at home in my free time. I would like to get out and explore the area, go for walks in the fields and in the mountains."

"They're not mountains, they're hills," one of the men said.

"Yes, hills. I believe I'll find some walking trails. I love to walk and watch the wildlife."

"Like bears?" someone asked.

Delia laughed. "Oh no. I hope I don't come across any of those. I was more thinking of birds. Maybe unusual and rare birds that people don't see much."

"I like birds too," Betty said.

"You do?"

"Yes. I saw a Golden-crowned Kinglet just last week."

"I believe they sing a sweet song."

"They do. That's how I knew what it was. They hang out in the conifers around here, and they're tiny, hard to see. You can visit us any time you like, Delia, when you get that horse and buggy," Betty said.

Delia was delighted that everyone was so welcoming. "Thank you. Does anyone know where I can buy a horse and buggy?"

Betty raised her hand. "I was reluctant to say, but I have a buggy, well, my husband does have one that he could sell."

"Really?"

"Yes. We were talking about it just this morning."

"That is good news."

"And we have an extra horse."

Samson interjected, "A horse you'd be willing to sell for the right price to the new schoolteacher?"

Joe was embarrassed at Samson's words, but no one else seemed to mind.

Delia laughed at Samson.

"Of course," Betty Marshal answered. "Joe, you can bring her up to our place tomorrow to look at the horse."

"I'd be delighted to do that."

"Really, Joe?" Delia asked.

"Of course. I just need some directions."

"I'll give you the address and write out the directions for you before I leave. I should be going. I didn't know it was getting so late."

"I'll get pen and paper for you." Joe headed to the back of the room, fetched a note pad and pen from a set of drawers in the corner of the room and passed it to Mrs. Marshal.

"Thank you. It's straightforward. You can't get lost."

Joe couldn't help smiling at the comment. He'd heard that so many times before. You can't get lost, or, you can't miss it, said by people who knew the way. Each time he'd heard it, he had gotten lost.

CHAPTER FIFTEEN

*W*hen all the visitors were gone a few minutes later, Delia pulled her coat on as she and Amy were leaving. "I can't believe how everything is falling into place. I have a place to live. Who knows what could be next? I'm sorry again about ruining the meal tonight, Joe. I really am a very good cook."

He chuckled, seeing the funny side.

She smiled, grateful he wasn't upset about the smoke or the repainting he'd have to be doing.

"Don't forget you're coming back to cook again," Samson called out.

"I won't forget. I'm happy you're letting me try again. You saved the day, Joe, with your toasted ham and tomato sandwiches."

Amy pulled her coat on. "The mustard on them was good."

"Yes, ham toasted sandwiches with mustard. They were delicious," Delia said.

"I think we were just all very hungry. Everything tastes

good to a starving man." Samson smiled at Delia. "I was so looking forward to trying out your cooking, Delia."

"Yes, so you keep saying."

Joe had to bite his tongue. Delia had not come there to cook for Samson, she'd come there to cook for him.

"I can come and cook again can't I, Joe?"

"Come back and cook anytime. You're always welcome."

"Thank you, Joe. I'll work out another time and let you know. It depends on when I can move in across the road," Delia said.

Samson sighed. "If you must be here too, Joe, you must. If you happened to be elsewhere when Delia comes back to cook, there'd be more for me."

Everyone laughed, except for Joe.

Delia moved closer to the door. "Joe, you don't have to take me tomorrow."

"I do. Once I say I'm doing something I carry it through."

"Oh, I hope I didn't put you in a bad position. I mean, if you didn't want to take me, but you felt you had to say yes anyway."

"I'm here as the bishop and that means I'm here to serve. Anyway, I have to make sure you get the right horse for you—be certain it's a good one and make sure the buggy is sound too."

"Thank you. I have no idea what to look for. I've never bought either. I've never taken too much notice of buggies, I just ride in them."

He smiled. "That's what I thought. You did a good job with the play with such short notice."

"It wasn't too difficult. I worked on it all day except for when I was burning the food."

"We should go now, Delia, it's getting late. *Mamm* and *Dat* will be waiting up for us. They won't sleep until we get home."

"I'm ready."

When they all walked out of the meeting building, Delia sniffed the air. "I still smell smoke. I'm so sorry, Joe. I must come back and clean those walls and wash the curtains to rid the house of the stink. It'll be the stinkiest house in Stinterton." She laughed loudly and on the still night air her voice was amplified.

"It'll be fine. You don't need to worry about anything. We'll fix it, won't we, Samson?"

"That's right, Delia. You just concentrate on your play."

"Thanks. I will." Delia felt a little better that they were taking it so well. If she'd done something like that at home, her mother would never allow her to hear the end of it. She got into the buggy with Amy and the two men stood and waved them off.

"Amy, I never would've thought there'd be two handsome men here to choose from. What do you think?"

Amy glanced over at her. "What do you mean?"

"You're single and so am I. Don't you think *Gott* put the two of them here for us—one each?"

"I haven't given it much thought."

"Well, think about it now. Which one do you like?"

Amy shrugged. "Both are nice. It's hard to choose between them."

"If you had to choose which one would you choose?"

"Joe I guess, but that's only if I would die if I didn't pick one."

Delia laughed at Amy. Now her decision was made, she'd get to know Samson better.

"What about you, Dee?"

Delia didn't want to upset her cousin. "Good thing you picked Joe because I say Samson."

"Okay."

"Amy, why are you being like this?"

"Like what?"

"Like you don't care about finding a husband. Don't you want a family some day?"

"I do. I'd love to have a family. I think of little else. I so want my own baby."

"Well, to have a family you need a man. Didn't your mother ever tell you that?" Delia laughed and by the gleam of the buggy light, she saw a smile touch Amy's lips.

"I'm not in a rush," Amy said.

"You will be in three years when you're my age. I wish I'd thought about it more years ago. That's what you should be doing. Take advantage of the men who visit. You said yourself there are no single men here, so it is reasonable to expect that your husband will be a visitor."

"That makes sense."

"I'm pleased you think so. Give it some thought. Don't waste your opportunities or it might be a long time before more visitors come. I hear you don't get many here. The bishop is trying to attract families to move here, not single people. Also this place is not somewhere you go on the way to somewhere else."

"You're right about that. Thank you for the advice, Dee. I will give it some serious thought."

"Good." Delia was pleased she could give her cousin some useful advice. "I'll just say one more thing. The older you get the less often opportunities come your way. It's so easy when you're young and everyone else is single. Then they start pairing off."

"I can see that would be a problem."

Delia had said all she could say. If her cousin didn't act on her advice there was very little she could do. She couldn't force her cousin into a relationship.

Since Amy wasn't talking as the horse clip-clopped down the dirt road, Delia closed her eyes and thought about Joe. Joe didn't care for her, he'd made that known a long time ago, so she hoped he would care for Amy.

CHAPTER SIXTEEN

*T*he next day when Delia hadn't heard from Joe as early as she'd expected, she borrowed her uncle's horse and buggy and headed to the bishop's house.

He had committed to take her to see the horse and the buggy that was for sale. It made sense to her to do it early in the day. He might not have things to do, but she still had the play to think about and helping her aunt and Amy with the chores. It made sense to get the journey over with in the early part of the day.

When she arrived where Joe was staying, she saw from the yard that there were only two horses when she recalled seeing three there the day before.

There was only one road to the place where she'd been staying, so she couldn't have missed him on the way. They would've crossed paths. She jumped down from the buggy, and hurried over and knocked on the door.

There was no answer.

She knocked again.

Not wanting to knock a third time, she looked through the closest window. She quickly jumped back when she saw Joe was coming to the door.

He opened the door, blinking, looking like he'd just woken up. His hair was all scruffy and his eyelids only half open.

"I'm sorry, did I wake you?"

He shook his head. "No. I had a sleepless night. Come in."

When she got inside, she became embarrassed for bursting in on him like this. He'd been kind enough to say he'd drive her, so she should've let him choose whether he'd do it morning or afternoon. Even though she was sure he'd said morning, so wouldn't that mean early in the morning rather than later? She looked at the clock on the mantle. "Oh, look at the time. I thought it was later than this. It's ten and I thought it was eleven."

"It's fine. I was coming to fetch you soon anyway."

"I figured as much. Do you want me to go?"

"No. I was waiting for Samson to return with the buggy."

"Where's he gone?"

"We had a problem with the oven. It won't turn on for some reason. We tried everything, but still—"

"Oh no! It's my fault, surely. I've broken it."

"I don't think so."

"I could've. So, where's he gone? I thought there were no other stores here. The next town is a hundred miles away or something, isn't it?"

"Not that far, but a fair distance. Mike said he sold someone a stove and they found they didn't need it and were bringing it back for a refund. Mike got them on the phone to see if they still wanted to return it and they said they are. Mike couldn't get away to fetch it for us, so Samson is picking it up."

"Okay. I should pay for it." She reached into her drawstring bag and pulled out a wad of cash. "I have this that I'm saving for the horse and buggy. I won't need all of it."

"Put the money away, Delia."

"No, I insist on paying."

"It's not necessary."

She sat down, pushing the money back into her bag, but instead it fell to the floor at the same time as tears trickled down her cheeks.

He frowned at her. It made him most uncomfortable when women cried. He felt dreadful. Taking a step closer, he asked, "What's wrong? I thought it would make you happy not having to pay for something."

"The bishop will know that I ruined his oven and made his house all smoky. I can still smell it, Joe."

Joe sniffed the air. "It's fine."

"That's because you've been here all night and your nose can't smell it anymore."

He sat next to her. "What can we do to make you feel better?"

She shook her head. "Nothing that I can think of. Bishop Luke will think so poorly of me. Then he'll tell my parents and they'll be so upset with me. My mother didn't want me to come."

"What about your father?"

"He thought it'd be good for me."

135

"While we're gone, we can open up all the doors and windows and the breeze will blow the smell away."

She looked out the window at the gray sky. "It might rain and if it does the rain might come in if the wind blows it at an angle."

"It might not."

She blew out a deep breath. "How long will Samson be?"

"I'm not sure, but we can take your uncle's horse and buggy. We don't need to wait for him since that one's all ready to go. Or I can hitch one of the other horses. It's not a problem."

"I didn't think of that." She looked up at Joe's reassuring face as he looked down at her. He'd been so kind. That was the first thing on her list—kindness. Perhaps he was the man for her, not Samson. Then she reminded herself that Amy liked Joe and that meant he was off limits.

"Feeling better now?" he asked.

"Much better. I'll be even better if we get back here and the fresh air has swept away the stale odor of smoke."

He laughed. "We'll rid of it." He stood up and reached out his hand. She put her hand in his and raised herself up. She stared up into his eyes for a moment, before she stepped away.

Her heart raced. They'd shared a moment of closeness. She was sure he felt something too.

Joe was shocked at himself. With her having a moment of being so sweet and feminine, his old feelings for her had flooded back. Then in another instant, he reminded himself of all the reasons he'd decided she wasn't the one for him. At times she was pushy, she was loud, she was domineering.

As he walked around the house opening all the windows, he had to admit she was also lively, and had a good heart. He also liked the way she interacted with children. She'd make such a good mother. "So, we'll take your uncle's buggy?"

"Yes."

"Ready when you are." He smoothed his hair down and put on his hat.

They walked outside and Joe closed the front door behind them.

Joe automatically took control and climbed into the driver's seat. She sort of liked that he automatically took charge instead of asking if he minded if he drove. But, it was her uncle's horse and buggy so she probably—maybe —should've driven it because she'd been the one to borrow it. None of that seemed to occur to Joe and she found she didn't mind.

CHAPTER SEVENTEEN

or the first five minutes of their journey, Delia couldn't work out if Joe was being a protective man by taking over the driving or whether he was completely insensitive. "Thanks again for doing this."

"It's my pleasure. I look forward to helping you. Now, if you're not sure about the horse or the buggy don't feel obliged to take either."

Delia bit her lip. "There aren't going to be a lot of choices around here, are there?"

"No, but you don't have to take the first thing you see. Others will come along. I'm sure of it."

She sank back into the seat and sighed.

He glanced over at her. "What's wrong?"

"Nothing. It's just that it's a big decision."

"That's why I'm with you. I know a lot about these things."

"Okay. I'm glad you've come with me." She looked out the buggy window at the dryness of the landscape. "We're badly in need of rain."

"It'll be snowing before it rains I'm guessing."

She looked back at him. "What will you do when you leave here?"

"I'll go back to doing what I was doing."

"And what do you do? I've never asked."

"I have a small store."

"I didn't know that. A store like Mike's parents'?"

"No. It's more of a workshop. We make barns, sheds and gazebos."

"I remember now. Someone told me you had a gazebo business. And, who's running it now?"

"I have good staff."

"You must make enough money if you can take so much time off."

He frowned. He didn't like talking about money especially when it was his own. He was starting to warm to Delia, even saw a possible glimpse of a future, but now he didn't know if she simply wanted to find herself a wealthy man so she could live a comfortable life.

"Did I say something wrong, Joe?"

"No, not at all. I do okay, but only because I worked hard for so many years to build up the business. It helps that I've got wonderful people working there."

"It sounds *wunderbaar*. It's such an achievement to work hard at something and actually see the results blossom before your eyes. Also, to bless other people with employment must be fulfilling for you."

He smiled. He'd never thought about it like that. Her words were sweet, but was that what they were designed to be? Was she simply buttering him up?

"You'd be a good boss to work for," she added.

Joe considered she was paying him too many compliments to be genuine. "I don't know about that."

"I think you'd be fair and honest. Of course you would be and what more do people want in a boss?"

"You wouldn't have a boss, would you?"

"I do. It's my parents. They're my bosses, each one of them." Delia laughed. "But really it's mostly the bishop or whomever he's appointed to look after the schools. In some communities it's a group of people."

"Parents."

"That's right, the parents. I hope I'm able to guide the children the right way to have the right behavior. Time will tell I suppose. I've only been doing it for five years."

"That's a fair time."

"I know. It's gone so quickly."

"It's good of you to come to such a faraway place. Do you think you'll be here for a long time?"

"I'm not sure. Wherever *Gott* takes me that's where I'll go. I'm sure He wanted me here."

"And why's that?"

"I just believe He had a reason for me being here."

Joe hoped she didn't think *Gott* sent her there to meet his cousin. She deserved someone so much better than Samson. He wanted to warn her, but couldn't think how without coming across as a bad person. When he realized he might not get another opportunity, he had to just tell her outright. "I hope you don't think He sent you here to find a husband because—"

"Joe Bontrager, I've never been so offended in my life. What makes you think I'd like you anyway?"

"Me? I don't. I wasn't meaning—"

"Stop!" She held up her hand at his face. "Best we don't talk about this again."

He breathed out heavily. He'd never been good at talking to women. They were far too emotional. Men were reasonable. At least you could talk to them and they'd let you finish a sentence. He tried again. "Delia, that's not what I meant."

"Please don't make things any worse." Delia turned her whole body away from him and looked out the window. A tear trickled down her cheek, and she couldn't wipe it away because Joe might see it. Best he think he meant nothing to her. She was silly to think a man like him would like her. No man had ever liked her enough to ask her on a third buggy ride.

She sat there, embarrassment heating her cheeks, for the remainder of the ride, wishing she'd never agreed to see this horse and buggy. She was in no mood to buy anything, or take any kind of advice from the man who'd rejected her for a second time. It was stupid of her to think a handsome man like Joe would like someone like her, but back at the house when they'd stood so close... it seemed like there was a chance. She was certain he'd felt it too, but it wasn't the first time she'd been wrong about Joe Bontrager.

CHAPTER EIGHTEEN

*W*hen they arrived at the Marshals' house, Delia quickly wiped her tears away and then joined Joe as they walked to the front door of the house.

"Delia, I'm not quite sure what I said to offend you," he whispered, while looking straight ahead.

"I'm not offended. I just said I don't want to talk about it anymore, and I don't."

He stopped walking and she turned around to face him. "I think we do need to talk about it."

"I'm not going to. Hush." She walked on ahead of him and knocked on the door. She felt immature and silly for the way she was acting, but she didn't need him to explain his rejection. There was no point in that.

Mr. Marshal opened the door. "Good morning. You found your way here then?"

"We did," Joe said.

"The horse is out in the field. Over this way."

They followed Mr. Marshall. "That's him there. Name's Ben."

"He looks good. When was the last time he was worked?" asked Joe. "He looks a little on the heavy side."

"Not for about six months or so, but I figured Delia wouldn't be taking him for long trips would you, Delia?"

"No, that's right. As long as he can make it back to the store in town. Because that's where I'll be keeping him."

"Oh, you've got no problems about that. He's been newly shod just last week."

"And is he used to traffic?" Joe asked.

"No horses are used to traffic around here." Mr. Marshal laughed. "We don't get enough to be concerned about. It's just used to the regular kind of cars and pick-ups, and Mike's delivery truck."

"That's good to know."

"Try him out if you like."

"Could we?" Delia asked.

"I'd be worried if you didn't."

"Will you do it for me, Joe? No racing him, though." She turned to Mr. Marshall. "Joe used to do harness races. Is that how you say it, Joe?"

"Close enough."

"Did you, Joe?"

"Yes, I did. I'm surprised you remembered, Delia."

"I'm not sure why." She hung her head, embarrassed. She should've kept her mouth shut.

"I won't go too fast. Don't worry about that," Joe said to Mr. Marshal.

"I wasn't worried. Let's get him hitched and you can have a drive of him, Joe. See how he is to handle."

"Let's do it," Joe said.

Delia watched as the two men harnessed the horse and hitched the buggy. Everything was pretty much the same as at home, no surprises, so she was certain she'd be able to manage on her own. Then she watched as Joe drove him up and down the road past the Marshals' house.

"He looks good," Delia said to Mr. Marshal.

"When he comes back, you can get a good look at the buggy. It's not fancy. It's not got heating in it or anything modern."

"I probably won't be driving it far so it doesn't matter. As long as the lights work, it'll be fine."

"They do, and it complies with all the safety measures."

"Good."

Joe came back up the driveway. "He drives well."

"Are you happy with him, then?" Delia asked.

Joe stepped down from the buggy. "I'm happy, yes, but are you?"

"As long as you are."

"What about the buggy?" Mr. Marshal asked. "Have a look inside, Delia."

Delia stepped past Joe and had a look at the interior. Everything was a little worn, but as long as that was reflected in the price, she was okay with that. "I'm happy with it," Delia said, "but I guess it depends on how much you're asking."

"Good question. How much?" Joe asked, taking over the negotiations.

Mr. Marshal named a reasonable price for both the

horse and the buggy and Delia immediately agreed and then said, "I left my money in the buggy. I'll get it."

While she was doing that, Joe and Mr. Marshall discussed how they'd get both the buggy and the horse back to Joe's.

Once Delia gave Mr. Marshal the money, Joe told her, "It's going to be a slow trip home."

"Yes, I'll take it nice and slow." Delia was excited to have her very own horse and buggy. And she was more than a little relieved she wouldn't have to be in the same buggy as Joe.

"We'll tow the buggy behind, and we'll lead the horse beside us."

Mr. Marshal said, "It'll be fine on these quiet roads. No trucks go between here and the bishop's house."

"Why wouldn't I drive?" Delia didn't like the sound of being in the buggy with Joe again. And had he said it would be a slow trip? That was even worse.

"The horse isn't used to the work," Mr. Marshal explained. "He's a bit out of shape, so we're making it easier on him. Once you get him back, just short slow trips to start with. Ease him back into things."

"Okay. If that's what you suggest." She could see their point. It would be easier on the horse if he didn't have to pull a buggy all the way home.

Once they had the buggy attached, they clipped a lead rope to Ben's halter.

As they drove away, they waved at Mr. and Mrs. Marshall who stood in front of their house to see them off.

Joe said, "We'll just keep the horse at my uncle's until you sort out something with Mike."

"Okay. Thanks for doing this, Joe. I didn't mean to take up your whole day."

"I'm happy to do it. I thought you might have some kind of plans this afternoon?"

"Oh, you mean the play? I've finalized it. I have to write out a copy for each person who has a speaking part. It wasn't good the other night when I had to tell people their lines before they said them."

"I can help you with that. My handwriting is clear and easy to understand."

"You'd help me write them all out?"

He smiled. "Of course. I'm here to help."

"Thank you." She looked back at the road ahead. "That's right. You're here to help as the bishop. Silly of me to think you would help as a friend."

"Hey, I'm doing it as a friend."

"Here to help, you said. I'm not stupid, Joe. I know what that means. People speak the truth even though they don't mean to sometimes."

He groaned and shook his head. "It's not—"

She held up her hand at him. "Stop! Don't speak."

"Stop cutting me off. I've a right to speak."

"Not if you're going to upset me, Joe Bontrager. Best we don't speak until we get back to your uncle's house."

"So you want to spend this whole journey in silence?"

She turned her body away from him and looked out the window, not bothering to answer him.

"Delia, you're the most stubborn frustrating woman I've ever met!"

147

She didn't move a muscle. He'd stop talking sooner or later if she didn't open her mouth. And she was right. They spent the rest of the journey in silence.

When they finally arrived back at the bishop's house, she said, "Thank you for taking me there and helping me buy the horse and buggy. I do appreciate it."

"You appreciate it, but you can't show me the decency to talk to me?"

She looked away. "I'll have Amy and my aunt and uncle help me copy out the scripts once I'm ready with the play."

His eyebrows drew together. "You're turning away the help I've offered?"

"That's right. I think you're too busy with all your duties. I don't want to take up any more of your time."

He shrugged. "It's not quite accurate, but if you want to behave like a child, like a disagreeable school child, I'll not stop you. Is that where you learned the silent treatment from, one of your students?" He hadn't even gotten a chance to warn her about Samson.

"No." She patted Ben and then unclipped his lead. "I'll see if Mike has got a pasture ready."

Joe stepped forward and grabbed the lead from her. "I'll put him in a yard here. We can sort things out in the morning. It's late and you must be tired."

He was right. She was tired, but only from spending the day with him.

She watched him walk the horse twenty yards away and let him out into a paddock. Then he walked back and proceeded to undo her new buggy from her uncle's. "There," he said when he was done. "You're free to go."

"Thank you again."

"No need to keep thanking me. Once was enough."

She climbed up into the buggy. "Goodbye, Joe."

"Bye." He stood and watched her leave, and then his cousin walked out of the house toward him.

"Hey, was that Delia?"

"Yes. I took her to get a horse and buggy."

"That's where you've been the whole day? You spent the day with Delia without inviting me?"

"That's right."

"You had a better day than I did, then."

Joe walked past him into the house. "I doubt that."

Samson walked behind him. "What do you mean? Not good enough for you to be alone an entire day with a beautiful woman?"

Joe stopped and turned around to face him. "That woman is as stubborn as a mule and as rude as a badger."

A smile tugged at Samson's lips and at that moment Joe felt ridiculous. "A badger, eh? Are they generally rude?"

"Yes." Joe stormed into the house. He was in no mood to talk after the day he'd had with Delia.

Undeterred, Samson wasn't finished with him yet. "Sounds like it's true love."

Joe took off his hat and tried to put it on the peg, but he missed it twice, so he threw his hat across the room. "Love? She won't even let me talk. She holds her hand up to my face and tells me to stop. How could I ever think about living with a woman like that?"

"Woohoo. Strong reaction for a man who has no feelings for the woman." Samson walked over, picked up the hat and hung it on the peg while Joe stood there looking on.

"I didn't say I had no feelings. We grew up in the same community. We lived not far from each other. I do have a certain fondness for her because of what we have in common."

"If you say so."

"I do." Joe headed to his room and closed the door. He slumped onto the bed and dissected his conversations with Delia trying to figure out what he'd said to upset her.

CHAPTER NINETEEN

*T*he next day, in need of getting out of the house, Joe walked across the road to the store. As soon as he walked inside, Amy and Delia pulled up in the buggy. He stood just inside the doorway and watched them. He wasn't happy when he saw Samson hurry across the road toward them.

Joe needed to check on what he was saying to them, so he headed back out the door and joined them.

"Hello again, Joe," Amy said.

"Hello. I'm happy to see you both again." He looked at Delia. "Have you brought your cousin to show her the horse?"

Amy laughed. "I'm not interested in horses. We've come to get a bag of flour."

"Cooking something, are you?" Samson asked.

"We're always cooking."

"Um, Delia, can I speak to you for a moment?" Joe asked, figuring she wouldn't say no in front of people.

She threw her head back and laughed. "Oh no. I'm in trouble it seems."

Samson laughed along with her. "Sure sounds like it. Don't take her too far away, Joe. I'm keeping my eye on you."

"Excuse us," Joe said, before motioning for Delia to follow him. As they walked down the road a little way, he could still hear Samson and Amy chatting. "I trust you're feeling better?"

"Yes, thank you. Oh, the horse feed. I'm so stupid. I didn't think to get any."

"I've enough. Well, my uncle has plenty. Just get some when you get around to it. I believe you can get that and everything else from Mike's store."

Delia locked eyes with him again, but this time she turned toward him. "That sounds lovely. I think that's a wonderful idea." She cleared her throat. He had a strange effect on her and she couldn't help being nervous around him.

Joe smiled, his stomach fluttering as he stared into her eyes. Maybe it wouldn't be so bad after all, he thought. Something told Joe there was more to Delia than what she presented to the world. He wanted to dig deeper, learn more about her. And to do that, he had to get her on her own. "I think we got off on the wrong foot somewhere, somehow. What if we spent some time together? Would you be willing to do that?"

Time alone together was a date, wasn't it? Her heart raced because she didn't want to explore a possible relationship only to end up disappointed. A date would lead to rejection number three, and could her heart take it? She looked back at Amy who had said she liked Joe. Was she stepping on Amy's toes? Amy seemed to be happily talking to Samson. She looked back at Joe. "I'm not sure that's a good idea."

He licked his lips. "I saw a grassy hill on the way back here yesterday. It'd be a perfect place for a picnic. There were even seats, and a roof in case the weather turns bad."

"Like one of your gazebos?"

"Similar, but not as nice as one of mine."

Delia laughed and relaxed a little. "I'd like that."

"It's about five miles down the road here."

Before he could make a time to pick her up, Samson yelled out, "Hey, Joe, great idea. Amy and I would love to join you on that picnic."

Joe was horrified. He had no idea Samson and Amy would've been able to hear him.

"Great! We can all talk about the changes I've made to the play," Delia yelled, the boisterous side of her personality rearing its head for the first time that day.

Joe's heart sank into his stomach. Why couldn't Samson take the hint he was trying to speak with Delia in private? It sure was rude to invite himself along, but it was already too late to say or do anything without looking rude and inconsiderate himself: two things that a man of God should never be.

"Don't you have work to do tomorrow, Joe?" Samson asked. "I could take these ladies myself."

"I'm sure we've all got other things we could be doing,

but we can take some time to enjoy our day." Joe paused briefly before saying, "I can plan for two extra people on the picnic." He hoped he didn't sound rude, but he wanted Samson to get the hint that he'd wanted to be alone with Delia. And he wanted Delia to know it too since she'd somehow got the idea he didn't like her.

"Then it's settled!" said Samson, smiling happily as he turned to Amy.

Joe and Delia walked back to Amy and Samson.

"I guess our plans have shifted a bit," Amy said. "I'll just get that flour, Dee. I'll be out in a minute."

"I'll help you. I need some things too."

"I'll see you again tomorrow for the picnic. We'll stop by and call for you both around noon? Does that suit?" Joe asked.

Delia's cheeks reddened. "Yes. I look forward to the picnic."

"Don't bring anything. I'll do it all."

"No, we have to bring something."

"It's my invitation, so allow me the pleasure of arranging every last detail."

Delia smiled. "Okay, since you put it like that." She gave him one last smile.

Joe watched as Samson rushed ahead and opened the door of the shop for Delia and Amy.

He stayed still to see if he could tell which woman Samson preferred. It was possible he liked Delia since he butted in and invited himself and Amy on the picnic.

The two women laughed at whatever funny thing Samson had just said in a voice that was too low for Joe to hear.

Could it be that Samson liked both women? Joe wondered how he would get time alone with Delia now that he wasn't going to be alone with her for the picnic.

When Samson entered the store behind the women, Joe headed back home, feeling a dark cloud overhead. Over the next few hours, he couldn't shake that feeling, no matter what he tried or what he told himself.

He finally went over the events of the day in his mind. How could Samson invite himself and Amy on his private picnic without at least talking to him about it first? Joe tried to keep his annoyance at bay the best he could, but sometimes the foolishness of others bothered him.

Joe had noticed Samson paid more attention to Delia at first, but then he did invite Amy to the picnic. What did Amy think of Samson? Did saying 'yes' to the picnic mean that she was interested in Samson? Not that it mattered either way, Joe thought, shrugging off the idea. Or did Samson like neither of the women particularly and had invited himself and Amy on the picnic just to give him a hard time?

Swallowing hard, he lay down on his bed and sighed. "Lord, please give me the courage to make it through this picnic, and the virtue to remain calm when things go awry. I trust in you and your guidance, my Lord. Please, guide me now." Joe did not like the feeling of having no control over things. Samson had always done these kinds of things to him.

As his heavy eyelids threatened to fall, Joe took one last look around his room.

When the darkness of the night engulfed him, a single thought put him at ease. Perhaps his uncle was right and he did need to find a wife. The quiet version of Delia could be exactly what he needed. Her company and affection would surely fill a void in his life. But, could he look past the part of her personality that was loud and occasionally brash?

CHAPTER TWENTY

When Joe's eyes slowly opened to the bright sun that shone into his drab room, he remembered it was the day of the picnic. At first he was pleased, but then he remembered that he and Delia would not be alone, thanks to Samson. He sat up slowly, letting his legs hang over the side of the bed before standing to his feet. He stretched his arms over his head and yawned.

As Joe got ready for the day, he thought about how he wanted the picnic to go. Perhaps Samson would afford him and Delia some alone time by taking Amy off on a walk or something of the sort.

When they'd been youths, Samson had always been a fast-talking, scheming child, finding his way to lead Joe and himself into trouble, then talking his way out of it and leaving Joe to get the punishment. They were both different, both thirty-year-old men now, but he was sure Samson hadn't changed too much.

The morning seemed to crawl by. Joe had gathered

food for their picnic, performed his chores, wrote half a sermon for next time and, then he noticed it was time to pick up the two women.

He walked into Samson's room figuring he'd slept in. His bed had been slept in because it wasn't made, but he was nowhere in sight. Joe walked outside and noticed that one of his uncle's buggy horses was also missing.

He didn't say he was going anywhere.

Joe couldn't work it out.

Had Samson forgotten about the picnic?

It wasn't likely because that was all he had talked about last night. Joe slipped his feet into boots, put on his coat and hat and then went to hitch the buggy.

When he finally moved the horse and buggy onto the road and the cold morning wind tickled his face, he forgot about Samson.

He inhaled deeply. The air was much different from home. Joe looked up into the gray sky and wondered if it might rain and ruin their picnic.

When the house came into view, he saw two women waiting just outside the front door. On drawing closer, he saw that the women were Amy and Mrs. Hostetler.

"Good morning, Joe," Mrs. Hostetler called out, waving happily as he pulled up his wagon.

"Good morning, Sylvia and Amy," he said, wondering where Delia was as he got down from the buggy. This would be an awful mess if Delia had backed out of the picnic. If he was forced to go alone with Amy, Mike would be most upset when he found out.

"It's a fine day; not too cold," Sylvia said, smiling as she looked up at the sky.

"Yes, it really is, but that's a wonderful thing since we're off to a picnic. Where's Delia?"

"Here I am," Delia said as she walked through the door.

At the sight of her, Joe's heart skipped a beat.

"And I'm sorry, Joe, I won't be coming after all," Amy said. "Please send my apologies to Samson." She looked over at the buggy. "Where is he?"

"Missing. I've got no idea where he is." Joe looked back at Amy wondering why she wasn't coming with them. He didn't want to ask. She wasn't ill if she was able to stand there smiling. She wasn't coughing and she didn't look pale.

The good thing was, he'd be alone with Delia just as he'd originally planned. He focused his attention on Delia. "Shall we go?"

"Yes." They said goodbye to Amy and her mother.

As soon as they got into the buggy, Delia said, "What's going on? First Amy pulls out and then Samson, or... I mean, it was the other way around."

"I know. It's weird. When I got up this morning I thought Samson was sleeping in and when it came time to go, he wasn't anywhere. Then I realized a horse and buggy were missing. Who knows where he is?"

"My horse and buggy aren't missing, are they?"

"No. They're our uncle's."

"That's so strange. I wonder where he's gone. Wait, what if he's going somewhere with Amy in secret?"

"That would be something like he'd do. He invited himself on our picnic and that's not good enough for him and he's stealing Amy away for a private picnic."

"No, that wouldn't be it. Now I think about it, Amy said she was not leaving the house."

"Why didn't she come with us?"

Delia shrugged her shoulders. "She said something about going to the store, so she will be leaving the house. She's told me two different things."

"The store, eh?"

"Yes."

He moved the horse forward.

"Now I'm intrigued about Samson and where he's gone."

"That's my cousin for you, unreliable and unpredictable. I still don't even know why he came here."

Delia looked in the back. "Where's the picnic food?"

He hit his head. "We'll have to stop by my uncle's. It's all prepared, but I left the basket of food on the kitchen table."

Delia laughed. "What about a blanket?"

"There's one in the back."

"Ah, I didn't see it."

"I doubt we'll need it because we can sit on the seats unless someone else has beaten us to them."

"I doubt that. I think the place you saw will be totally deserted especially seeing it looks like rain."

When they eventually arrived at the picnic spot, on top of the hill in the location where Joe had planned, he noticed a lone horse and buggy. "Looks like we've found the missing—"

"He's here? Oh, look, he's over there under the tree."

Joe pulled up the buggy and saw Samson sitting on a

blanket under a spreading tree, and not at the table and chairs.

This was a fine mess.

Now he wouldn't have Delia alone and Amy wasn't here to occupy Samson.

All Joe wanted to do was get to know Delia better. If he'd known they wouldn't be alone, he would've talked to her on the way there.

Hopefully, Samson would leave when he found out Amy wasn't with them. "I've got no idea what he's playing at. Why wouldn't he wait so we could all go together?"

"I guess we might find out."

"Something tells me we won't. Oh well, looks like we're having a picnic for three." Joe got out of the buggy and took the basket of food from the back of the wagon, and then he and Delia walked over to Samson.

"You're missing one," Samson said.

"I'm sorry, but Amy changed her mind about joining us," Joe said.

"Why's that?"

"She couldn't make it today. She's sorry," Delia said, offering Samson a weak smile.

Samson frowned and pushed back his hat to scratch his forehead. "Well, that's just wonderful. I carefully planned the sweetest, nicest time for her that I could think of, hoping she'd actually see me for the man I am. What a fool I was." He let out a sigh.

Joe frowned at him. He planned the sweetest time? What part of any of this was his idea at all? Joe looked around and couldn't see that Samson had brought anything to the picnic besides the rug on which he sat.

Delia sat down beside him. "You're not a fool." Delia touched Samson's arm.

Samson looked at Delia and smiled.

Ah, Joe thought. It's Delia that Samson likes and he's going about it by pretending to like Amy. It's the kind of thing his devious cousin would do.

With hands on hips Joe stood there watching their interaction.

"How did you know we'd planned to come to this very spot?" Delia asked.

"Ah, simple. I just drove until I found a gazebo-like structure. I didn't think there'd be two around here."

"So you overheard my private conversation with Delia?" Joe asked.

"Yeah, you know I did. That's how I found out about the picnic. I wasn't going to wait for an invitation that might never come."

Giving up, Joe set down the picnic basket and laid out the food. Joe then sat on the blanket after Delia helped him unpack. The longer Samson and Delia spoke, the more Joe worried that they were getting along too well.

"Excuse me," Joe said, clearing his throat as he did so. "But may I join the conversation since we're now a party of three instead of four?"

"Of course!" Delia raised her eyebrows. "I didn't know we were leaving you out."

"You don't have to ask to join the conversation, just do so," Samson said. "You're not four years old anymore, are you? You used to be so timid. I thought you'd changed, but I might've been wrong." Samson laughed. "Do your students also have to ask to speak, Delia?"

"Not really. They know they can't speak until question time."

Samson laughed again. "Okay. Now it's officially question time. You can speak now, Joe. Don't hold back."

"I'm fine," Joe said.

"As you please." Samson turned to Delia and started talking again.

Anger churned in Joe's stomach. Couldn't Samson see he was in the way? Joe breathed out heavily to let go of the anger. He knew he shouldn't have feelings such as the ones he was having and he did his best to ignore them.

For over an hour, Samson and Delia were locked in a lively conversation, talking about everything from the weather to her family at home. It bothered him that Delia spoke so freely to Samson when she was never like that with him.

Feeling defeated, Joe hoped to salvage the picnic in any way he could. It seemed that a change of topic was more than necessary, so he thought about his uncle's place and the upcoming Christmas festivities.

He had no idea what the two of them were talking about now as he'd stopped listening some time ago. He broke into their conversation when he heard a pause. "How are you doing with the play, Delia?"

"It's coming along fine," Delia said, looking at him only briefly before returning her gaze to Samson.

"I think the play sounds like a pain in the neck, but I'll help as much as I can." Samson laughed loudly at his own words. "I hope you don't mind me inviting myself to help, do you?"

"Of course I don't. Joe offered to help me write out the

copies now I've officially finished, so you can help too if you want."

"I'd be delighted."

Joe felt his body warming as agitation boiled within, but he calmed himself again and offered the happiest smile he could. "Anything that is worth doing takes time and effort. I'm told this Christmas play is an important event for the entire area."

"It sounds like it," Delia said.

Samson frowned and pushed his hat back slightly on his head. "Can we talk about it another time, Joe? I think I've had enough of picnicking for now. I might call in on Amy and see how she's doing."

Delia rested her fingertips lightly on Samson's arm. "Do you have to go? We've barely started the food and you haven't eaten much."

"I had a big breakfast." Samson chuckled. "Let me know when I can help with that writing, Delia."

"Oh, I will."

Wasn't it Delia who Samson preferred? Then why was he visiting Amy? Or did he want both women to want him? Joe's stomach churned once more at the way Delia and Samson smiled at one another.

"Okay. You best be on your way, then, Samson," Joe said, glad for some time alone with Delia.

"Thank you both for the lovely picnic." Samson stood up.

"But you hardly ate a thing." Delia looked at all the food still on the blanket.

"I wasn't hungry. Someone took my mind off eating." Samson smiled lovingly at Delia.

She smiled back and then looked down. "Oh, your blanket. We're sitting on it."

"Take it with you, Delia. It'll give me a reason to visit you."

CHAPTER TWENTY-ONE

*D*elia and Joe sat in silence as they watched Samson walk away.

"So, that was a bit unexpected," Delia said.

"You didn't seem to mind him being here."

Was Joe jealous? "I felt sorry for him. He thought he'd see Amy and she didn't come."

"He shouldn't have just come here. It's no way to treat a lady. He should've brought Amy here. We should've all come together."

"But, Joe, perhaps he was hoping to take Amy home alone. So they could have a private time together to talk."

"Hmm, that does seem likely. He is a scheming fellow."

Delia frowned at him for saying something mean about his cousin.

Reading her face, he responded, "Don't look at me like that, Delia. You don't know him like I do."

Then the rain fell from the sky out of nowhere. Delia looked up. "See? You made Gott cry."

He laughed. "Don't say that."

"You're the one who shouldn't say things. Don't say mean things about your cousin."

Joe stood and packed up the rest of the picnic food into the box. "Is it better if I merely think them, and then you don't know him for what he is? Better for you to be warned."

"Oh, don't say that, Joe. He seems so nice."

"See? He's fooled you already."

Delia didn't say anything more while she helped Joe pack up the food. Once they were done with that, they both worked together to fold the large blanket. Then with Delia holding the blanket under her arm, and Joe carrying the picnic basket, they hurried back to the buggy while large raindrops splattered onto them.

Once they were both seated, Delia lifted the hem of her soaked dress. "I'm wet through and through."

"Me too." He looked over at her. "Suits you, though."

She smiled at his compliment. "I don't know how."

"It makes your face sparkle."

Delia looked away, embarrassed. The ride home was spent in silence while Joe wondered if he should say more, but nothing came into his head. It wasn't an awkward silence. It was a comfortable and serene quiet.

As soon as Joe pulled up his horse at the Hostetlers', Delia jumped down from the buggy. "I'd better get into dry clothes. Thanks for the picnic, Joe. I really enjoyed it."

"I'm pleased you had a good time."

"I did, I did."

"I'll walk you to the door. Delia, I didn't get a chance

today to say some of the things I wanted. It was hard with Samson there. Can I see you tomorrow again?"

"Oh. I just want to go over the play one more time."

He hung his head. "That's understandable. Well, don't forget I'm helping with writing out copies for the actors."

"I won't forget, I'm just worried about not having enough time."

"You'll do it."

"I keep thinking I've finished, but then when I read it over again, I want to change it. I'll get it finished and I'll let you know."

"No, Delia. Leave it the way it is."

"You think so?"

"I do. I honestly thought it sounded pretty close to perfect the other night."

"Thank you. Maybe you're right," she said.

"I am. Just be confident that it's good, because it is."

When they got to the door, Mrs. Hostetler met them. "Hello, Joe. Coming in?" She looked them up and down and her eyebrows rose.

"No, thank you, not today. We got caught in the rain and I'll have to get out of these wet clothes." He handed her the parcel of food. "I've some extra food for you. I hope you can make use of it."

"Oh, thank you, but surely you two boys can use it?"

"We have too much already. I overdid it with the food order." He handed Mrs. Hostetler the food, and then looked to see where Delia had disappeared, but couldn't see her. He figured she might have gone around to the back door to take off her muddy shoes before going into the house.

169

All along Delia had thought that Joe was a nice person, and that was why she had been so sad to have lost him all those years ago. Now, she'd seen another side of him completely. He had been awful to his cousin today.

CHAPTER TWENTY-TWO

*I*t wasn't until Saturday that Joe heard from Delia next.

He was delighted that both Delia and Amy knocked on his door, and he was even more pleased that he'd beaten Samson to the door.

Delia stood there waving some pages in the air. "I've finished and I hope you're happy with it."

"I think it's wonderful," Amy said. "I read the whole thing."

"I liked it before," Joe said as Samson elbowed him out of the way.

Samson stood in front of Joe. "Please come in and sit by the fire and warm yourselves." He ushered the young women in and over his shoulder, he said, "Joe, get them something hot to drink."

Joe narrowed his eyes. "Coming up. What will it be?"

"Nothing for me, thanks," said Amy.

"I'll have a black coffee please but only if it's not too much trouble."

"I've only just made some. I'll be back in a minute."

He came out of the kitchen with two mugs of coffee. One was for himself, and he handed the other to Delia.

"Where's mine?" asked Samson.

Joe wasn't happy. He'd used up the last of the brewed coffee and he wasn't going to be away from Delia any longer than he had to. "This is yours." He handed his over to Samson.

Amy said, "We have Christmas play costumes from years gone by, and the painted props for the backdrops. We have a backdrop that shows an old city and fields, and I'm pretty sure we've got some backdrops for the inside of a home."

"Perfect. I think that's all we'll need for your play," Samson said.

"Hmm, same costumes and backdrops belonging to a different story. I hope no one minds." Delia warmed her hands around the coffee mug.

Samson shook his head. "No one will. Sounds like they've had the same Christmas story every year for the past ten years. They'll be pleased for the variety." He gave Delia a big smile which didn't escape Joe's notice.

"Joe, it's Christmas in ten days, if we count today. Amy tells me the play is always the Saturday night before Christmas and this year Christmas day falls on Monday. We must have the full-dress rehearsal on Thursday night and everyone will need their lines as soon as we can get them to them."

"I'll make it happen, Delia, don't worry." Joe smiled at Delia.

Samson said, "I'm free today if you want help writing them out."

"I'm glad you offered. If the four of us can do that today. We'll have them written out in no time. There are six actors with speaking parts so all we need is for us to write them out three times each, because I've already written out four copies of the play, in addition to my own."

"I'm ready," said Joe.

"Me too." Samson reached out his hand, and Delia handed everyone a copy of the play and extra blank sheets of paper.

"Be sure to write clearly please."

Joe sprang to his feet. "Let's do this at the kitchen table. I'm sure it will be easier to work there."

When Delia walked in, she was pleased to see it was all back to normal. "Oh, Joe, it doesn't smell at all and… you painted the room?"

"I did."

"With my help," Samson added.

"Hey, all you did was find the tin of paint in the barn."

"I supervised."

Joe rolled his eyes.

They were an hour into their writing when a loud knock sounded on the door. Joe got up to answer it and saw Mike standing there. "Hello."

"I saw an extra buggy here and wondered if Delia might be here."

"Yes, come in."

Joe walked him through to the kitchen.

"Hello, everyone."

173

Once everyone had greeted him, he said, "Delia, we will have the wiring taken out of your place tomorrow. You can move in any time you wish after that."

Delia dropped her pen. "That's such good news. Thank you!"

"Yeah, well, we managed to find someone. It's the same fellow who's fixing the freezer for us." He looked down at all the pages on the table. "What are you all up to?"

"Writing out copies of the Christmas play."

"Ah, I look forward to coming to that." He looked closer. "Seems you need a stapling machine to keep the pages together. Do you have one here, Joe?"

He shrugged his shoulders. "I haven't seen one around."

"I'll go and get one you can use. We always have a spare in the store."

"Thanks," Joe said.

Amy jumped to her feet. "I'll come with you. It'll save you coming back here."

"Okay, thanks."

Amy and Mike walked out.

Delia couldn't help wondering if something was going on between Mike and Amy. They seemed very friendly, always finding time to be with each other, grabbing moments here and there. As she was deep in thought about them, she felt Joe looking at her. She looked over at him, and he smiled at her and then looked away. He resumed writing.

CHAPTER TWENTY-THREE

*T*he day of the play arrived and Joe was looking forward to it, but only because he'd see Delia. Amy told Joe he couldn't even watch the dress rehearsal they were having, but Samson was allowed because he was an extra in the play.

Joe stood outside the building, hoping Delia wasn't developing feelings for his cousin. It ate away at him. When everyone started arriving for the night, including quite a number of local Englishers, Joe merged with the crowd and headed into the meeting hall.

He sat down two rows from the front. When many of the seats were filled, Samson rushed up to him.

"Joe, it's starting in five, Dee said."

"Great. Break a leg."

Samson frowned at him.

"What?"

"You have to announce the play and do whatever it is you're supposed to do."

He gulped. "Me?"

"Yes. You keep telling me you're taking Uncle Luke's place, so do it. He'd normally get up."

Samson was right. Joe kept an eye on the clock on the wall until it reached seven, and then he stood up and moved to the middle in front of the curtain.

He stood there and looked around at the sea of eyes and faces as they turned to look back at him. Pushing aside the drama of Samson turning up unexpectedly, Mike's feelings for Amy, and Delia's odd behavior, he began, "I want to welcome everyone here tonight for our yearly Christmas Play."

Everyone clapped, and the smiling faces of the crowd put him at ease. He drew a deep breath to steady himself.

"As some of you may know Bishop Luke is still in Ohio recovering from a buggy accident."

Everyone sighed and a few murmurs moved through the audience.

Joe raised his hands. "But don't worry. He's healing okay and he'll be back here again in no time."

Everyone clapped.

He soon saw that the crowd was easy to please.

"This year we have a very special woman who's helping with the play. It's Delia Kauffman, who's also our community's new schoolteacher. I'd like to thank all the actors and everyone helping with the play." He hoped he wasn't forgetting anything. Or was he talking for too long? "Please enjoy…" No one had even told him the name of the play, "this year's Christmas play."

Everyone clapped and then he sat back down. The overhead gaslights dimmed and the curtain parted.

CHAPTER TWENTY-FOUR

*J*oe looked around for Delia to tell her how pleased he was with how the play had turned out. A man forgot his lines, but he soon recovered from it when the other actor covered for him. That was the only hiccup. The crowd had loved it, evident from their lengthy and enthusiastic applause when Delia and the actors came onstage together after the last scene.

He soon saw Delia disappearing out the door with Samson, and that made anger rise within him.

Samson had to know how he felt about Delia and he was trying to capture her heart right underneath his nose.

He followed them and when he stepped outside, he saw them disappear around the corner of the building. Joe kept advancing, stopping just before the corner because he could hear them talking.

"Not me?" he heard Samson ask.

"No, I'm sorry."

"Why not?"

"Joe just feels familiar and safe. He feels like home. I don't know how he feels about me, but…"

"That makes no sense. Joe's not who you think he is. He's an actor, like someone acting a role in a play."

Joe wanted to confront him, but he kept quiet so he could hear how Delia responded.

"That's not true."

"Take my word for it. I just don't know what you see in him. What *do* you see in him?"

"Don't tell him."

"I won't. I'm just interested to know what's attracting you to him."

"Apart from him being handsome, smart, hard-working and a nice person, it's hard to put into words."

"Hmm. So, he doesn't know how you feel?"

"No. That would be awful. When I'm around him, I get so nervous I can hardly speak, so I speak too much. Then I'm sure I do and say everything wrong. I get loud or say something outlandishly stupid."

Joe listened some more. What she was saying explained so much.

"Are you sure he's worth all these tears?" asked Samson.

Tears? Joe put his hand on his heart. She was crying… over him?

"Maybe the tears are for myself."

"How so?" Samson asked.

"I don't know. I'm so confused."

"Yes, I know, you're confused if you like Joe rather than me, you are confused that's for sure."

"Don't say that."

"He's not worth it, Delia. Trust me."

"I think he is."

"If you're not going to change your mind about me, you need to tell Joe how you feel."

"Oh no, I could never do that."

"I heard him asking you on that picnic, so that must mean something. He wouldn't have done that if he didn't like you."

Was Samson actually trying to help matters now after first saying such awful things about him?

"It wasn't like that. He didn't ask me to the picnic because he liked me. We had a misunderstanding and he wanted to straighten things out."

"You don't have to go on a picnic to do that. Do you want me to talk to him for you?"

"No. Don't you dare. I'd die of embarrassment if he knew how I felt about him."

"Well, one of you has to make a move, and I think he's made it."

"What do you mean?"

"He likes you and he's shown it, but you're so unsure of yourself that you can't see it."

"No. He said some things, so I dare not say anything. Also, what you don't know is that when we were younger we were closer, but then he rejected me. He…"

"He might regret that now. Talk to him and find out."

Delia laughed. "I'm not so good with talking to grownups. I prefer the company of children."

"You have to if you ever want a chance with him."

"I don't know. What should I do, or say? I wouldn't have a clue."

SAMANTHA PRICE

"Why don't you say you enjoyed the picnic and ask him if he'd like to go on another?"

"In the snow?"

"Ah, yes, the snow. One minor detail I overlooked."

"It's no use. Things never work out for me. After our family moved away, I saw him at weddings but he never even said hello to me. He showed no interest whatsoever, not even a tiny bit."

"That was dumb of him. That was in the past. Now he knows you a little better, and he knows you as a woman and not the girl you used to be."

Joe was amazed. Delia was hiding herself inside the brash exterior she used as a wall of protection. He'd so often caught glimpses of the real woman inside, but hearing her words just now... it melted his heart. And, Samson—this was a different side of his cousin and one he'd never before seen.

When the headlights of a taxi turning in the driveway made a long shadow out of Joe's silhouette, he hurried back to the entrance of the building.

He watched to see who'd get out of the taxi. It was a young woman, who got out with a small suitcase. It was his duty as the stand-in bishop to greet her.

When he walked forward, he saw it was Becky Yoder, the woman Samson had dated. "Hello, Becky, nice to see you again."

"Hello, Joe. I heard you were filling in for your uncle."

"That's true. What are you doing out here?"

"I've come to surprise my fiancé."

He tried to conceal his shock. For lack of anything

180

better to say, he asked, "Oh, and who's that?" He knew very well who it was. Why else would Becky be there?

She laughed. "Samson of course."

"Let me take your suitcase."

"Thank you." She handed it to him. "Could you possibly find someone who'd take me in for a day or two while I'm here?"

He frowned. "It'll be more than that with Christmas day being on Monday."

"*Jah*, you're right. It'll be a week, I guess, but no more. I know it's not convenient, but I just missed Samson so much that I had to be here. I've come to surprise him."

"Let's get inside," he said, as gentle snow fell again from the sky. "He'll be surprised all right." Joe went back over the conversation he'd overheard. He had missed the first bit, but Samson must've told Delia he liked her, for her to say what she'd said. It caused anger to rise in Joe that a man who was betrothed would talk to another woman like that. A conversation with Samson had to take place.

When they walked in, she looked around. "Where is he, Joe?"

"I'll find him for you. Meanwhile, have something to eat. We've just had a Christmas play, that's why there are so many people here."

"Thank you. I would be happy to eat something."

Joe hurried outside, knowing he'd have to interrupt Samson and Delia's conversation. Thankfully, he didn't have to because he saw Samson walking toward him through the snow by himself, and Delia was nowhere to be seen. He marched up to Samson. "You have a woman you're going to marry, Samson?"

Samson froze and his eyebrows rose just slightly. "It's true. Who told you?"

"Why were you going on picnics with Amy and Delia? Flirting with them and saying nice things?"

Samson shrugged his shoulders. "I'm not married yet. I had to be certain Becky was the one for me."

Joe shook his head. "It sounds disrespectful to me. The idea is to make sure she's the right one before you ask her to marry you."

"Hey, I don't need to be lectured by someone like you."

Joe was annoyed with himself for almost forgiving his cousin. He hadn't changed one bit. "Does Becky know you're doubtful?"

"No, and don't you tell her. I love Becky, but I just wanted to be sure. I don't think there's anything wrong with that. Anyway, one's in love with you and the other one is having some secret liaison with Mike."

Joe spluttered. "Mike?" He knew he was talking about Amy.

"If you'd been doing your job better, you would've noticed Amy is disappearing all the time and ending up somewhere with Mike."

"Your fiancée is inside."

"What?" Samson's eyes grew wide.

"She just arrived in a taxi."

His eyes bugged out. "Becky's here?"

"Yes."

Samson hurried past Joe into the building, passing Mike who was walking out.

Joe followed Mike around the side of the building where, standing in the snow, he saw Amy waiting for the storekeeper. They fell into an embrace.

Joe walked up and cleared his throat loudly, causing the couple to spring apart.

"Joe!" Mike said.

"What's going on here?"

"I told you I have feelings for Amy."

"You did? You told him that?" Amy asked.

Mike ignored Joe and turned to Amy. "Yes. I've loved you ever since I laid eyes on you when you moved here five years and four months ago. I talked to Joe about how we could make this work. If you want to stay in the community, I'd be willing to join, but please say you'll marry me either way."

CHAPTER TWENTY-FIVE

*T*ears streamed down Amy's face. "I will, Mike, I will." She threw her arms around his neck and the couple hugged as more gentle snow sprinkled on them from above.

Joe didn't know what to do. He respected their love even though they were from two different worlds. They'd make it work if both were willing.

He turned around and headed back inside, knowing he might get the blame for this relationship when it became public. Maybe Thomas would think it wouldn't have happened if Uncle Luke hadn't left, or perhaps it would confirm his uncle's belief that Samson would've done a better job as his stand-in.

Regardless of what others might think, Joe couldn't help smiling at the heart-warming scene he'd just witnessed.

True love was a miracle from God. Seeing Mike and Amy had given him the same feeling as watching a foal being born, or seedlings popping their head above the earth on their way to maturity.

He looked around for Delia. When he couldn't find her, he asked if anyone had seen her. Someone said they'd seen her leave.

He was disappointed. She hadn't even said goodbye. He was even more annoyed when he saw Becky and Samson staring lovingly into each other's eyes.

Something wasn't right. He couldn't wait another day to set things right with Delia and tonight, romance seemed to be in the air.

He had to reach her before she got back to her aunt and uncle's. There was no time to hitch a buggy, he grabbed a bridle, put it on the nearest horse and jumped on him bareback. He often used to ride bareback when he was a boy. Now he galloped the horse down the dirt road in the direction that Delia would've gone.

When he rounded a corner, he saw buggy lights and hoped and prayed this was her buggy. Then the buggy slowed and stopped. He slowed his horse to a walk and then drew level with the buggy. When he saw it was Delia, he jumped down.

"Joe, what are you doing?"

"You didn't say goodbye."

"I did look for you, but couldn't see you anywhere."

"You left without Amy?"

"I couldn't see her either. Aunt Sylvia said she could go home with them. I was tired."

"You look like you've been crying."

"I'm okay. Anyway, what are you doing on that horse?"

He walked closer. "You did a wonderful job with the play."

Her cheeks turned pink and she turned away. "Thank you." When she turned back, she said, "Did you know your cousin is getting married?"

"I just found out. I'm sorry if you thought… you and he…"

Her jaw dropped open. "Oh no. Not for a moment. Oh, you thought I liked him? No."

He smiled. "I was trying to warn you about him that day on the way to buying the buggy."

"Oh."

"You thought…"

"I did. I left without helping with the cleaning. Is it okay if I go back to help clean up tomorrow? I was too tired to do it tonight."

"I'd love you to come back tomorrow."

"You would?"

"There's something you should know."

She frowned at him. "What's that?"

"I wake up every morning wondering if I'll see you that day."

Her eyes opened wide. "Oh, Joe. You shouldn't say things like that."

"Why not if it's the truth?"

She put her hand to her throat. "What are you saying?"

"I'd like to spend more time with you, if you'd be all right with that."

A smile turned her lips upward. "I think I'd be okay with it."

"That's good enough for me."

She nervously touched her prayer *kapp* strings.

"Did you know Amy and Mike have something going on?" he asked her.

"I was a little suspicious, but she never said a thing. What's happening?"

"They're very close."

"Oh. I hope she'll tell me about it."

"I've got an idea everyone will find out about them soon. I just overheard Mike asking her to marry him."

"Really?"

"Yes. Then Becky arrived to be with Samson."

"*Jah*, I saw her getting out of a taxi. I put two and two together. It's all happening."

"Love is always around at Christmastime, I've found."

She smiled. "Shall I drive you back to your place?"

He bent his knees. "Yes please! I'm not as young as I was last time I rode bareback."

Delia laughed. "Clip the horse onto the side and we'll lead him back."

"Only if I drive."

Delia rolled her eyes and moved over.

When they got back to his uncle's place, most of the people had gone home. Only two buggies remained. He led the horse back into the paddock and then walked back to Delia as she was sliding back into the driver's seat.

"Thanks for bringing me back."

"I don't know what the urgency was. You could've talked to me tomorrow."

Pangs of guilt rippled through him. He had to be

honest. "Delia, I heard what you said to Samson. I know you have feelings for me."

Delia opened her mouth and didn't know what to say.

He continued, "I feel the same about you. I'm thinking I should never have let you go back then, all those years ago."

"I can't believe you'd do a thing like that. It's not right to eavesdrop."

"I didn't mean to and I'm sorry, sort of, but in truth I'm glad I did. I was confused about how you felt about me and now that I know…"

"Just wait a minute. Now you like me because I like you? What if another woman confessed to liking you, would you then like her?"

"No, of course not because she wouldn't be you."

"Just like the chicken."

"What do you mean?"

"You don't care about women like you didn't care what part of the chicken you'd like for dinner. Each woman is the same as another, just like the chicken."

He hung his head, remembering the first time he ate at her uncle and aunt's place. They had all been disturbed because he didn't have a preference for a certain portion of the chicken. "That's not so. I'm sorry you feel that way about me."

"Well, am I wrong? If I'm wrong tell me so and I'll be corrected." Her whole body trembled with annoyance. "I can't work you out. You like me and then you don't like me. Years later, you don't like me and then you do, but only because I like you." She took hold of the reins. "Goodbye, Joe."

"No, wait, Delia."

"I can't be with a man who thinks one woman is as good as another. You're just like your cousin. I found out what he was like tonight when his fiancée showed up. You Bontrager men appear to think every woman is the same, one as good as the other. I'm not going to be anyone's convenience. I won't be back here tomorrow." She moved the horse and buggy away from him.

He walked after her, keeping level with the slow-moving buggy. "You think you're a convenience? Well, that's hilarious because you're not. You're the most inconvenient, hard-headed, stubborn woman I've ever met."

She slapped the reins hard against the horse's rump and then Joe was left talking to himself.

CHAPTER TWENTY-SIX

*J*oe walked back to his uncle's house dragging his feet. When he got inside, he saw people including his disreputable cousin and Becky, Samson's fiancée, who was clueless about the kind of man Samson was. He knew he'd have to tell Becky about Samson's flirting ways, but not tonight. They were staring lovingly into each other's eyes. Joe couldn't believe how Samson had disrespected Becky. Joe didn't say a word to anyone when he walked past them to his room.

He closed the door.

Normally, he would've locked up the meeting room and made sure it was empty of food so vermin wouldn't be encouraged, but tonight he didn't care.

Now he knew he'd never make a good bishop. His life was too out of control.

It was his own fault. He never was one to want to follow the rules, only following them enough to get by. Now he regretted that because all he saw for himself was a lonely life of nothingness.

He'd worked too hard getting his business up and running, ignoring having a personal life and a woman to share everything with. Mistakenly, he thought a woman would appear when the right time came. He was wrong. The years of being alone had taught him how rare a good woman was.

Had he ruined everything between him and Delia? Because he'd rejected her all those years ago, she had trouble believing he wanted her. He had no idea how to make her see he'd been a fool. But if they couldn't see eye to eye on that small point, would that mean they'd always suffer miscommunication?

Joe fixed his sheets and then lay down. He stared up at the ceiling as his heavy eyelids closed. As the darkness engulfed him and his conscious mind began to leave, a sharp pain struck his heart as an image of Delia flashed before him. The shock of it all sent him right back to the waking world.

Sitting up with a shortness of breath that he couldn't explain, Joe panted for a few moments.

Something wasn't right. Thoughts of Delia came back to the forefront of his mind, but it was the question that came next which really got him rattled.

If only Delia didn't have such annoying ways. Could I live with a woman that loud?

Then he remembered she said she was nervous around him and that made a ton of sense. In fact, it explained a lot.

His mind wandered to Delia's soft, creamy skin and piercing eyes that captured his attention whenever she was near.

As he wrestled with a blanket to warm the shivers from his skin, Joe lay back down and tried to sleep once more. His second attempt was circumvented when a single question stood out amongst the many.

That was when it hit him. This was all a deliberate setup, wasn't it?

The blackness of night and the chilling sound of creatures in the woods caused Joe to sit up once more. His mind felt like a battlefield, with various thoughts and ideas at war to decide what he should believe.

His mind went again to the setup and he thought about that some more. Delia had been sent here as the schoolteacher, and he'd been sent to stand in for his uncle in his bishop duties. It never made sense why they'd sent him and not Samson, the more favored nephew, but now it did. Uncle Luke knew Samson was betrothed and he must've known about the plot to set him up with Delia.

Another question rattled in his head.

Was Delia a part of the plan? Had she put herself forth to be set up with him?

If she knew about it, she was deceiving him and he couldn't be around a woman who'd do that to him.

"Lord, I know we speak often and I have never asked you for any selfish desires in all the years since I've come to know you, but I seek your advice and wisdom in a time of uncertainty and confusion." He held his hands together on his chest as he prayed.

"Is Delia the right choice for me? Should I follow my heart and get to know Delia, or would that be a path of folly?"

Joe felt tears welling in his eyes and he quickly wiped

them away as he said, "Amen," and rolled onto his side. It was now in God's hands, and if any angels or guardians were watching over him, then perhaps they could shine some light on the darkness of uncertainty that lingered over his life.

Everything would've been so much easier if Samson hadn't shown up. He couldn't think straight with that annoying man around.

CHAPTER TWENTY-SEVEN

The next morning, Joe was roused from his sleep when a thin stream of light shone brightly through the window, falling directly over his eyes. Without thinking, he sat up sleepily and rubbed at his face before standing to get ready for the long day ahead.

Joe was pleased it was morning. Now he'd no longer toss and turn wondering about whether Delia knew about the plot to match them together, and he thought some about what he'd say to Samson's fiancée.

First thing, he had to make Delia understand that he liked her.

When he stood up, he was inspired with a good idea. Since Delia was a schoolteacher and used to reading things, he'd write all his feelings down on a piece of paper and have her read it. At least that way, she wouldn't be able to interrupt him. It would be like a letter, except he'd hand deliver it so he'd be sure she'd read it.

If she didn't want him after that, at least he would've tried everything. After he changed, he walked out to the kitchen and made himself a cup of coffee. When he had found a sheet of paper and a pen, he sat down at the kitchen table wondering where to start.

Joe had no idea.

He didn't want to raise the past by explaining why he'd ended things between them years ago. And neither did he want to discuss their recent disagreement.

Instead, he decided to write all the feelings he had for her—all that was on his heart. As soon as his pen touched the paper, it all poured out of his heart.

He ended the one-page note by telling her he wanted to spend more time with her and then he asked if she'd forgive him for all past wrongs. If so, they could look forward to a new beginning.

He had his pen poised to sign his name just as his cousin walked into the room, yawning. Joe managed to hide the note under the coffee pot before Samson could see it. "I thought you'd be sleeping in. It's Christmas eve and there's no meeting today."

"I know that, genius. Now that Becky's here I'll have to get a Christmas gift for her."

"You should've had that sorted weeks ago."

"I got a gift for her, but I left it with my mother to give her. I didn't know she'd be here. Now, I don't know what to do. I'm hoping to find something at the store across the road, get some gift paper and ribbon, maybe make a pretty bow and put it on top."

"I can't get my head around the fact that you would come here like you did, as though you have no woman in your life."

"What are you talking about? Becky didn't mind me coming here."

"I'm talking about you flirting with Amy and Delia, going on picnics, seeking them out for private conversations, confessing your feelings for them."

Samson pushed his hair away from his face. "I was just seeing if there was anyone else out there for me."

"But you've done this twice before—called it off two weeks before weddings."

"I'm not calling it off and it's not two weeks before the wedding."

"I know that. I'm not saying it is two weeks before."

"I wouldn't have come here if I knew you'd judge me like this. Judge not lest ye be judged. Ever heard of that?"

Joe pressed his lips together and stared at his cousin. "I think Becky should know you were uncertain." He just wanted Samson to be accountable for what he'd done.

"Justice Joe!" Samson laughed out loud. "I love that. Suits you perfectly. Hey, Justice Joe, make me a coffee, would you? Then you can talk at me all you want."

Joe didn't let Samson bother him. He picked up the coffee pot and headed over to fix some more coffee. Then he looked up and saw a buggy heading toward the house. "Seems everyone's out and about early this morning."

"Who is it?"

Joe looked harder. "It looks like it's your fiancée, with both Amy and Delia. I wonder what they're doing here so early?"

"Becky stayed with them last night."

"I didn't know."

"I'd say my woman misses me, and couldn't wait to see me. She's brought the others along for the ride."

Joe moved out of the kitchen.

"Hey, what 'bout my coffee?"

Joe ignored him, and walked outside. When the buggy stopped, a red-faced Becky got out. She was followed by Amy, and then Delia, who looked withdrawn and demure. Something was going on. Becky walked straight past him as though he wasn't even there.

Joe guessed Becky had found out the kind of person his cousin was.

"Good morning everyone," Joe said, as cheerfully as he could, hoping his brightness would wash over on the girls.

Becky was nearly at the front door when she turned around to face him. "Good morning, Joe. Is Samson awake yet?"

"Sure is, he's in the kitchen."

"I'd like to talk with him in private if I might."

Joe was taken aback. "Certainly."

When she entered the house, Joe looked at the two young women. "What's going on?"

"I had to tell her the truth about something," Delia said. "If the situation was reversed I'd want to know what I told her."

Joe knew exactly what it was about. He wasn't the only one who was upset by Samson. "It's cold out here. Let's sit on the porch. It'll be warmer."

When they got there, they were still shivering so Joe peeped inside and when he saw the couple were talking in the kitchen, he ushered Amy and Delia in to sit beside the fire.

Joe couldn't help being pleased his cousin was being told off, but why wasn't he hearing any cross words or maybe some shouting?

Samson and Becky walked out of the kitchen with huge smiles on their faces. "Samson said he'll make everyone pancakes," was all that Becky said.

Joe was amazed Samson had either been able to lie or talk his way out of his problems.

It fell into place when Joe saw Becky clutching the letter he'd written for Delia. He didn't know what to say, so he said nothing and walked into the kitchen to finish making the coffee.

Then he overheard Becky telling the girls about the beautiful letter Samson wrote for her asking for forgiveness and promising a bright future.

His cousin had done it to him again.

Joe recalled hiding that letter under the coffee pot when Samson had walked into the kitchen, yawning his head off. Then he'd forgotten and moved the pot to make fresh coffee. To make matters worse, Joe hadn't yet signed it and neither had he addressed it to Delia in any way because he had intended to hand it to her himself.

Samson rattled around in the saucepan cupboard.

"What are you doing? That was my note to Delia."

From his crouched position, Samson looked up at him. "Your note you say? I saw no name on it."

"So what?" Joe was not going to allow him to get out of this one. He had to be held accountable for the deception. The only hesitation Joe had was that Samson would put a spin on the story to make Joe look bad, while he'd come off smelling like a rose.

Samson continued, "I thought I might have gotten up in the middle of the night and written it in my sleep."

"Are you sleep-writing notes now?"

"It seems a likely explanation. People do many things in their sleep. That note shows my true feelings for her."

Joe couldn't believe him. Even when faced with the truth, he lied. "You'll have to tell her."

"No, I'm not and neither are you. What makes you think I'd tell her? What reason could I possibly have?" Samson stood up and looked Joe in the eyes.

"I'm telling her now."

Samson grabbed Joe's sleeve. "Please don't. I'm not as good with words as you are and that note said all that I wanted to say. Women like that kind of thing."

"Yeah, and you know that because you've had two fiancées, no wait, three."

"I'm remorseful. I take it all back."

Joe reefed his arm away from his cousin. Now, he felt slightly sorry for him. What if he was truly in love with Becky? He didn't want to ruin things for them.

And, besides that, he wasn't sure if he should tell Delia about the letter after all. The note revealed he wanted to make a commitment to her, but he didn't if she had done some deceiving of her own. Some men wouldn't mind that kind of thing but for him it was a deal breaker. In a woman, he needed honesty and transparency above all else.

Joe sat down at the table as his cousin made pancakes, still deciding what to do. "I think the truth needs to come out here."

"The truth about what?" asked Amy who had just walked into the kitchen.

"It's something to do with Joe," Samson said as quick as a flash.

Joe dropped his head into his hands. He knew this would have a huge backlash on him.

"What truth Joe?" Amy asked.

CHAPTER TWENTY-EIGHT

*J*oe raised his head and lowered his hands, and now saw the other two women had come into the kitchen, and all eyes were pinned on him. He looked down at the table. "Samson?" Joe waited for him to say something.

"All right. Becky, that note wasn't meant for you. It was meant for Delia."

She looked at Samson, utterly confused and stunned. "You're not in love with me, you're in love with Delia?"

"No, I wrote it," Joe said.

Delia opened her eyes wide. "You wrote that lovely note for me, Joe?"

"I did. Now that I'm being honest about that, you can be honest with me about something, Delia. Did you know about the setup between you and me?"

"I'm not sure what you're talking about."

"You don't have to be too bright to join up the dots to know what's happening around here."

"What are you talking about?" Delia frowned.

"You come here as the new schoolteacher. The bishop bypasses his favorite nephew and asked me, an outcast, to replace him. Why?"

Delia shrugged. "I guess you'll have to ask the bishop why he chose you instead of Samson."

"I'm his favorite, that's what you think?" Samson asked smiling.

Becky walked out of the kitchen and Amy went with her. When he saw them leave, Samson followed. Now Delia was alone with Joe.

She sat down in front of him. "So, you think someone is trying to match us together because we both landed here at the same time?"

"Yes."

"How could you upset me so much? You think there's something going on and I knew about it? Do you think I was involved in some kind of deception to win you over?"

"No, but it crossed my mind you might've known about it. Did you?"

It was too much for Delia. "You or Samson can drive Amy and Becky home. I need to leave right now." She hurried out of the kitchen and then he heard the front door close.

From her reaction, Joe knew she had nothing to do with it. The thing with the letter had gone far better than he'd expected, so why couldn't he have kept his mouth shut about the setup?

He followed her. "Where's Delia going?" Amy asked.

"She's upset. It's my fault."

Amy walked over to him, shaking her head. "You men! What did you do?"

He gulped. "I had this crazy idea that someone was setting us up, Delia and me. I thought maybe that Delia knew about it, and I asked her."

"Oh, Joe. What you thought is true, but she didn't know anything."

He felt dreadful and hurried to the front door to catch Delia before she left. Amy followed him, talking some more. "Your parents and my parents had the idea and when the bishop had his accident and Delia was coming here anyway, asking you to come here was a perfect idea to get you two together."

"The bishop's in on it?"

"Yes," she called after him as he ran toward the buggy that was heading down the driveway. He made a leap and grabbed the door, opened it and climbed in beside her.

Delia reacted in fright and stopped the buggy. "Please don't."

"Amy told me everything just now. She told me what I said was true, but you knew nothing about it."

She frowned. "We were set up? My job's not real?"

He took a deep breath. "I believe your job is real, but Amy said my parents and her parents had the idea to get me here with you. Then they enlisted the bishop's help after the accident."

"Why would they do that?"

"I have no idea. Well, it seems someone thought we'd be good together."

"Your parents like me?'"

"They do."

"I feel such a fool. For everything I've said to you. And… you really wrote that note for me?"

He smiled. "I did. And I didn't give Samson permission to use it. I wrestled with whether to tell anyone or to keep having Becky believe he wrote it, but in the end I figured—"

"You figured the truth should come out."

"Exactly."

Delia nodded. "I agree. That's why I told Becky the truth about Samson and how he was acting like he did not have a girl he was betrothed to, back home. She acted like she didn't believe me, but maybe she did. Either way, she wanted to talk with him about it."

Joe smiled. "Seems we think alike about a few things."

"Yes, we do when it comes to what we think is right." She turned her body toward him a little more. "That was a nice note, Joe. I remember most of what you wrote. I will put the past behind us."

"You will?"

"Yes."

He was relieved. "That makes me very happy. I think we should pay a visit to your aunt and uncle to find out who was behind this arrangement. Let's get the full story."

"Yes, I'd be interested to know, but do you think we should have something to eat first?"

"No. I really don't want to be near Samson right now after what he did."

"I don't blame you. I can't wait to get my letter back and read it properly." She looked down at the reins. "Um, shall I let you drive?"

"You can drive, that's fine. We don't have far to go."

Delia sent up a silent prayer of thanks. God, and a few other people, had wanted her to come to Stinterton, and now she and Joe were together. It was a better outcome than she could've dreamed.

It was a miracle.

She glanced over at him, scarcely believing how quickly all her prayers had been answered. Joe gave her a big smile and it quickly melted her heart.

WHEN CONFRONTED with the questions Delia and Joe put to them, Thomas and Sylvia admitted to what had taken place.

"Joe, your parents and the two of us thought you two would make a good pair. We discussed you both at length."

"But you'd never met me. Delia and I are trying to work out how it unfolded. And how do you two know my parents?"

Thomas and Sylvia looked at each other. "Well, because of Delia's parents."

"Aw, no. My parents were involved too?"

Her aunt and uncle nodded. "They were the instigators. When the bishop was told, he immediately agreed to help with whatever was needed."

Joe was a little upset that he truly wasn't the bishop's preferred choice. His uncle probably would have preferred Samson after all.

Delia was deflated. "I'm so sorry, Joe."

"Don't be. They've all been in it together." Joe shook his head.

"But it worked." Thomas gave them a wink.

Delia and Joe looked at each other and laughed.

CHAPTER TWENTY-NINE

he next day was Christmas Day and the Hostetlers had invited Joe and his cousin to Christmas lunch.

They sat around the table feasting on a large roast turkey with all the trimmings, fried chicken, ham and cheese casserole, a mix of oven-roasted vegetables, mashed potatoes with gravy, sauerkraut, and an assortment of green vegetables.

Samson asked a question, "So, Thomas and Sylvia, can you tell me what happened between Joe and Delia? Were you really in cahoots with Joe's folks to match him with Delia?"

"It's true," Sylvia said, "and we don't think there's anything wrong with that."

Thomas smiled, seeming highly amused about something.

"Two lost hopes, eh? Did you think, why not put the two lost causes together, they might make a match of it?" Samson laughed at his own words.

Joe frowned.

Delia laughed. "Oh, thanks very much, but I don't think I was a lost cause and neither was Joe."

"I don't know quite what to say about that. It would be a different thing altogether if they said we'd be a match because of this or that. Why did you or my folks think we'd suit each other?" Joe asked.

"Like we told you and Delia yesterday, Joe, it was your personalities. You're both very similar."

Delia and Joe looked at one another. Delia said, "I would think we're—"

"Exact opposites." Joe finished her sentence.

"It turned out well didn't it?" Thomas asked.

Delia shook her finger at Uncle Thomas, pretending she was mad. "That doesn't excuse what you did."

Thomas laughed as he helped himself to more ham and cheese casserole. "You don't seem like you're too unhappy about it."

Joe said, "No, just not pleased with the way you went about it. It could've been embarrassing and nobody likes to be—"

"Fooled," Delia said, finishing the last word of his sentence.

Joe smiled at Delia. "It's not so bad, is it? If they hadn't done that we never would've found each other again."

"'Again?'" Samson asked. "I didn't know you two had a history together."

"I thought I told you," said Joe.

"Oh, really? I probably wasn't listening."

"Ancient History," Delia told Joe with a small hand-swipe through the air as if to brush it all away. "I guess we can forgive them all, can't we?"

Joe nodded. "Maybe we can, seeing it's Christmas Day."

Samson smiled at Becky. "You did a great job with the meal."

She laughed. "It wasn't just me. We all helped. The three of us."

Sylvia said, "Yes, with three other women in the house, I'm able to put my feet up while the girls take over for me."

"Well, I think we'll be leaving in a couple of days, won't we, Becky?"

"Yes, we will, and then we'll have to arrange the wedding."

Joe was amazed that Becky had forgiven Samson. She'd shrugged the whole thing off—everything he'd done. Joe then chose to put everything to do with those two out of his mind. He looked over at Delia, still amazed that he'd rediscovered her.

After lunch was over, Amy asked her parents, "Can I visit Mike? I said I'd see him and his parents today."

Thomas said, "Sure, I don't see why not. What do you think Sylvia?"

Sylvia nodded. "Okay, but don't be too long. You can go after the washing up is done."

"I'll do that for her," Delia said.

"And I'll help," Becky added.

"Thanks a bunch, you two!" Amy stood.

"That's some heavy snowfall, I don't know if you should go."

"I can take her," Samson offered.

Joe had a suggestion. "Why don't you and Becky both go for a drive and take Amy to Mike's? I'd be happy to help Delia clean up here."

"Oh, Joe, we can't have you do that." Sylvia's mouth turned down at the corners.

"I insist. You and Thomas go relax in front of the fire."

Soon, Delia and Joe were alone in the kitchen clearing plates and placing the leftovers into containers to be squeezed into the gas-powered refrigerator.

"Don't you think it's funny how my aunt and uncle are okay with Amy and Mike?"

"Not really. Seems he'll join our community. He's going to be talking to my uncle about it as soon as he gets back."

Delia shrugged her shoulders. "It's good for Amy, but my parents wouldn't be so lenient."

"What will your family think about you and me?"

"Oh, they'll be happy enough. Remember, they were behind the plot."

Delia was rinsing off plates under the running water. She and Joe had admitted to liking each other and now it was clear they were 'together,' but their relationship hadn't been defined. Nor had it been talked about whether Joe would stay in Stinterton or go back home. If he left, they'd have to write to each other and, in her mind, that was no way to develop their relationship.

"You're quieter than usual," he said as he placed more plates beside her. "Do I hear wheels spinning in your head?"

"I'm just thinking how much I love this time of year. I

love watching the snowflakes fall, and I even love the cold because it's so cozy when you're getting warm."

"Me too, I love it also. It's the first Christmas I've been away from my family."

She turned around to face him. "It's the first time I've been away from my parents, too."

He swallowed hard. "Where do you want to be next Christmas?"

"Anywhere, as long as I'm with you."

He smiled and took hold of her hand.

She pulled back. "My hands are wet."

"I don't care." He took hold of her hand again. "Delia, we've had so many misunderstandings, missteps, and misstarts. I don't want there to be any misunderstandings again, so…" She wasn't focused on him. He saw that from her face. "Why do you look so worried?"

"I'm just wondering if missteps and misstarts are real words, and how one would spell them."

He laughed. "Forget you're a teacher for one moment, will you? Look at me." She looked up into his eyes and he wanted to reassure her. "There's something about you that draws me to you."

She waited for him to say more, and saw he was waiting for her. "I feel the same way about you, always have."

"I want you to come back with me, Delia. I know you've got your heart set on being the teacher here, but my business is back home and it's not practical to be in a place like this."

She gasped and opened her mouth. "Are you asking me to marry you?"

That hadn't occurred to him. He'd pictured them being together and getting to know each other—thought she'd move to his community and they'd see how things went, but as soon as she said it, it felt right. "I am."

"I can't believe it." She threw her arms around his neck and hugged him.

He whispered in her ear, "Delia Kauffman, will you be my wife?"

"Yes, I will, Joe Bontrager."

Warmth flooded through his body. He wrapped his arms around her and desperately wanted to kiss her. It would be their very first kiss.

"I'll be Mrs. Bontrager."

He chuckled. "I hope you like the sound of that."

"I do, very much."

"I'm pleased I'm able to provide you with a satisfactory last name."

She smiled as she rested her head on his shoulder. He kept his arms around her, loving that she was a perfect fit. "Let's get out of here."

"We've got all this to do."

"We'll get through it, and then we'll spend some time on our own. I don't care how cold it is outside."

CHAPTER THIRTY

When Samson and Becky came back with the buggy, Delia and Joe took it out again.

As they moved the buggy down the road, Joe glanced over at her. "Are we doing this, are we really getting married?"

"We are, because you said yes and I agreed." She giggled. "Or something like that. Anyway, I'm not letting you change your mind." Faith had prevailed. God did have a man for her in Stinterton just like she had believed.

He glanced over at her. "I don't want to. Don't you change yours."

She moved to sit closer to him and tucked her hand around his elbow. "I won't."

"I'm not leaving you here. I'm taking you with me when I go home. They'll figure out what to do about a teacher, I'm sure."

"I hope no one will be angry with us. I suppose they won't because of the setup being their idea." She laughed. "Maybe there's some other couple that needs to be brought together like we were, another single school-teacher."

Joe laughed too. "Exactly." He stopped the buggy at his uncle's place, making sure the horse and buggy were under cover.

"Why are we here?"

"Come inside. I've got something for you." They got out of the buggy and hurried inside to get out of the falling snow. "Sit down."

She sat on the couch, rubbing her arms up and down. "It's cold in here with no fire."

"I'll light one."

A few minutes later, the fire was crackling. She got up and moved closer to the hearth, standing with her back to it while he disappeared into one of the bedrooms. He came out a minute later with something behind his back. "Close your eyes."

"Why?"

"Just do it."

"What have you got there?" She moved to one side in an attempt to see what was behind him.

"Close your eyes and you'll find out."

Finally, she closed her eyes.

"Okay, open them," he ordered.

When she opened her eyes, she saw a tiny black and white kitten curled up in his hands. "Joe! She had the babies?"

"Yes, and she had them in my room. I left the closet door open and she had them on one of my pullovers that she must've pulled off the hanger."

"They're a few days old because this one's eyes are

open. How many are there?"

"Come see for yourself."

She took the kitten from him and cuddled it before she walked into his room. The cat was now happily sitting in a wooden box inside the closet that was filled with old cotton shirts. "How many?"

The cat looked up at her and purred, seeming pleased with herself.

"Four." She crouched down and put the kitten back with its mother and stroked the proud mama from chin to chest, earning a louder purring. "Kitty, you're so clever to have all these babies. I'll make sure they all find good homes. Perhaps we'll find a vet around here because you can't have kittens all the time. These ones are so nice, though."

"That one's for you, if you'd like it."

She stood up. "For me?"

"Yes. It can be our first pet."

"Oh, Joe. That's the best Christmas present ever. I will call him or her Misty. I think that's a lovely name for a pet. I don't have a gift for you. I feel dreadful."

"Don't. I don't need anything."

She lowered her head. "There's just been so much happening, so much to think about."

"We don't exchange gifts in my family. I called the bishop earlier about the kittens. He wants me to find homes for them, and he said he'll be back as soon as he can."

"Good." Delia looked down at the kittens. "One is gray, one is nearly all black, one nearly all white and one black and white. What made you choose that particular

217

kitten for me?" Delia sat on the floor in front of the box and Joe crouched beside her.

"It was the adventurous one. The first one out of the box exploring. It reminded me of you."

Delia smiled. "I don't know that I'm adventurous."

"I think you are, and brave." He stood up and lifted her to her feet. "Let's call our parents and tell them we're getting married."

Delia couldn't keep the smile from her face. Now it seemed more real. "Okay, if you're brave enough."

"I think I am. I'll have my folks find a place for you to stay because I'll want you to stay somewhere close by. I want us to be married as soon as we can. What do you say?"

"I agree."

Joe pulled her toward him. "That's the very best Christmas present you could've given me."

They looked into each other's eyes. Joe lowered his mouth to hers and they shared their very first kiss.

A YEAR LATER, Joe and Delia were back in Stinterton. They'd been married ten months, and they were back for Amy and Mike's wedding. Mike had joined the community and the bishop had allowed him to keep the store running just as it was, as long as he lived simply in a house with no electricity.

Not long after Delia and Joe had left Stinterton with Misty, Delia had dropped some large hints to the bishop and his wife and even offered to pay for their cat to be neutered. Eventually, they agreed and took Kitty to the vet to prevent her from having more babies. In a small town such as Stinterton finding homes for cats was a problem.

Samson and Becky were marrying in one week's time, so Joe and Delia couldn't stay in Stinterton very long as they had to travel back to attend their wedding.

Delia and Joe were glad that the 'two-weeks before the wedding' milestone had passed. They were confident Samson would go ahead with his third attempt at getting married.

While they were in Stinterton, and for old time's sake, they went back to the picnic spot where they'd been a year before.

Delia carefully stepped out of the buggy, and Joe soon joined her, putting his arm around her.

"Are you too cold?" he asked.

"I'm perfectly fine." She loved the way he fussed over her. He was everything she'd hoped for in a husband. In fact, he had ticked all the boxes on her list.

"Do you know what I found out?"

"What?" she asked.

"We'll be here for the Christmas play and they're going to be doing your play again this year."

"Mine about the Samaritan?"

"Yes."

She couldn't help smiling. "That means they must've liked it."

"I'd say so." He looked around at the rolling hills. "Remember the day we came out here?"

Delia laughed. "I think we had an argument or two."

"No, not exactly. We came out here when I was trying

to make up for the argument you thought you were having with me, but you were really having with yourself."

She laughed. "You make no sense sometimes."

He sighed. "Another Christmas in Stinterton. I never thought we'd be back here, not for one moment."

"*Gott* works in wonderful ways, his miracles to perform."

He pulled her closer. "Stop worrying. We'll get our miracle. Just relax about it."

She opened her mouth to say something but he placed his finger on her lips.

He continued, "We haven't been married a year, so you're worrying about nothing."

"But Joe—"

"I won't listen to another word."

She took hold of his hand and placed it on her belly, and his eyebrows drew together. "We're blessed already, Joe."

"We are?" he stepped back and looked at her midsection.

"Yes. It's only early days. I found out before we left. I wanted to tell you when it was the right time. I wanted to wait for a special moment."

He stood staring at her.

"Aren't you happy?" she asked him. "Or are you angry I kept it from you for a day?"

A smile touched the corners of his lips. "I'm more than happy. There are no words to describe how I feel right now."

She saw tears glistening in his eyes.

"You've changed my life so much, Delia. Better in

every way, and now we're going to be parents. We're going to be a family with more than just Misty." He pulled her toward him and hugged her. "We thought last Christmas was the best we ever had. I say it's this Christmas that's our best yet."

Still with her head against his shoulder, she said, "And then it'll be the best one ever, come next Christmas, because we'll be holding our baby."

"Thank you for saying yes to marrying me and not giving up on me."

"It wasn't really me. We can thank all the people who pulled the strings to bring us together. Do you think we'll be doing that for our children when the time comes?"

"I'd hate to think that we would."

She raised her eyebrows.

Then he added, "But if they are as hardheaded as the both of us, I think we might have to."

"That's true."

They stayed locked in each other's arms while Joe silently thanked God for their past, their present, and their future.

Thank you for reading Amish Bachelor's Christmas.

www.SamanthaPriceAuthor.com

THE NEXT BOOK IN THE SERIES.

A Blessed Amish Christmas

The very day Adam Fisher decided to propose to Charity, a disturbing letter arrived that made him doubt everything Charity had told him.

Adam and his family had brought Charity into their hearts and their lives.

Was it all a lie? Most disturbingly, he'd even trusted her to look after his daughter.

Charity had fallen on hard times and had learned to seize opportunities. This time, has she taken things too far?

Will it take a child to show these two lonely hearts the true meaning of love, forgiveness, and... Christmas?

ALL SAMANTHA PRICE'S SERIES

Amish Maids Trilogy
A 3 book Amish romance series of novels featuring 5 friends finding love.

Amish Love Blooms
A 6 book Amish romance series of novels about four sisters and their cousins.

Amish Misfits
A series of 7 stand-alone books about people who have never fitted in.

The Amish Bonnet Sisters
To date there are 28 books in this continuing family saga. My most popular and best-selling series.

Amish Women of Pleasant Valley
An 8 book Amish romance series with the same characters. This has been one of my most popular series.

Ettie Smith Amish Mysteries
An ongoing cozy mystery series with octogenarian sleuths. Popular with lovers of mysteries such as Miss Marple or Murder She Wrote.

Amish Secret Widows' Society
A ten novella mystery/romance series - a prequel to the Ettie Smith Amish Mysteries.

Expectant Amish Widows
A stand-alone Amish romance series of 19 books.

Seven Amish Bachelors
A 7 book Amish Romance series following the Fuller brothers' journey to finding love.

Amish Foster Girls
A 4 book Amish romance series with the same characters who have been fostered to an Amish family.

Amish Brides
An Amish historical romance. 5 book series with the same characters who have arrived in America to start their new life.

Amish Romance Secrets
The first series I ever wrote. 6 novellas following the same characters.

Amish Christmas Books

Each year I write an Amish Christmas stand-alone romance novel.

Amish Twin Hearts
A 4 book Amish Romance featuring twins and their friends.

Amish Wedding Season
The second series I wrote. It has the same characters throughout the 5 books.

Amish Baby Collection
Sweet Amish Romance series of 6 stand-alone novellas.

Gretel Koch Jewel Thief
A clean 5 book suspense/mystery series about a jewel thief who has agreed to consult with the FBI.

Made in the USA
Monee, IL
14 January 2023

25325059R00135